PRAISE FOR

On the Bright Side

"I laughed until I cried and then laughed and cried some more." —David Suchet

"Thoughtful, entertaining, and wise. Long may he live." —*Minneapolis Star Tribune*

"Humorous... A realistic and perceptive glimpse into the aging process, shaped by empathy, optimism, and vibrant wit." —Booklist

"Highly entertaining... Wise and witty, his musings are thought-provoking and relevant to everyone regardless of age, and his delightful and charming personality will win over readers everywhere... *On The Bright Side* is the diary of an extraordinary man who lives an ordinary life. He makes an impact on almost everyone he meets, and seeks to understand the crazy world in which he resides. His clever commentary and madcap adventures will leave a long-term impression... Hendrik Groen is an unforgettable and absolutely spectacular character who readers will wish they could befriend." —*Book Reporter*

"Delightful... Groen strikes just the right note here with his wit and ironic observations... So warm, touching, and funny that you don't have to be a member of the Old But Not Dead Club to enjoy it."   —*Library Journal* (Starred Review)

"A worthy read... Darkly funny... thought-provoking, moving, and so pertinent to our times... Hendrik and some of his fellow residents form a delightfully rebellious Old But Not Dead Club, [and] the group's joie de vivre is contagious... Their friendships are likely to make you chuckle as well as move you to tears."   —*Winnipeg Free Press*

"Another amusing, enjoyable, and eye-opening read... Hendrik's bluntness is just a part of his memorable voice and the book's undeniable charm... With its dry wit and its random observations, *On the Bright Side* is alternately quirky and profound. It's more than just an entertaining read; it's sure to give you a new love and respect for octogenarians."
                                                        —*Nights and Weekends*

Enjoy Groen's light touch but do not be fooled by it...*The Secret Diary* is a handbook of resistance for our time."

—*Express* (UK)

"Funny and frank—a story with a great deal of heart."

—Graeme Simsion, *New York Times* bestselling author of *The Rosie Project*

"A story about how friendship, selflessness, and dignity lie at the heart of the human experience. When I'm an old man, I want to be Hendrik Groen."

—John Boyne, internationally bestselling author of *The Boy in the Striped Pyjamas*

"Funny, tragic, and sometimes heart-rending."

—*Het Parool* (Holland)

"Hendrik Groen is king. My mother, 78, suffers from dementia. Doesn't read a newspaper or magazine anymore, only old photo albums can grab her attention for longer than 5 minutes. Hendrik made her laugh out loud, and she was reading for a good half hour."

—Ray Kluun, author of *Love Life*

"Hendrik Groen is a heart-warming hero."

—*Trouw* (Holland)

"With pungent phrasing, Groen takes down life in a retirement home. Both charming and hilarious. Four stars!"

—*Leeuwarder Courant* (Holland)

"Groen's day-to-day worries in a retirement home are just as hilarious as the diaries of Adrian Mole."

—*Zin Magazine* Debut of the Month

"Tears were streaming down my face—from laughing so hard. I couldn't stop grinning for three days."

—*Ouderenjournaal* (Holland)

"Never a dull moment with my new BFF Hendrik Groen."

—Read Shop, Hedel (bookseller)

"It reminded me of a combination between *The Hundred-Year-Old Man Who Climbed Out of the Window and Disappeared* and *One Flew Over the Cuckoo's Nest*. Wonderful! Shame it's finished already."

—Arjen Broers, Bookshop Bruna (bookseller)

"Heart-warming, funny, and poignant. It's about all aspects of life. EVERYBODY should read this."

—Bookshop Stevens (Bookseller)

Two Old Men and a Baby

Or, How Hendrik and Evert Get Themselves into a Jam

HENDRIK GROEN

Translated by
Hester Velmans

GRAND CENTRAL
PUBLISHING

NEW YORK   BOSTON

Copyright © 2019 Peter de Smet and Meulenhoff Boekerij bv, Amsterdam

Translation copyright © 2020 by Hester Velmans

Cover design by Elizabeth Connor. Cover illustration © Christina Allen. Cover copyright © 2021 by Hachette Book Group, Inc.

Grand Central Publishing
Hachette Book Group
1290 Avenue of the Americas, New York, NY 10104
grandcentralpublishing.com
twitter.com/grandcentralpub

First US GCP Edition: June 2021

Grand Central Publishing is a division of Hachette Book Group, Inc. The Grand Central Publishing name and logo is a trademark of Hachette Book Group, Inc.

The publisher is not responsible for websites (or their content) that are not owned by the publisher.

Library of Congress Cataloging-in-Publication Data has been applied for.

ISBN: 978-1-5387-5352-1 (trade paperback), 978-1-5387-5351-4 (ebook), 978-1-5387-5456-6 (library)

Printed in the United States of America

LSC-C

Printing 1, 2021

Two Old Men
and a Baby

Tuesday, December 21, 2004

1

"Where the hell are those angels now…"

For just a second, the woman's face twisted into a scowl. Then her steely smile was back. Two children stared up at her. Only the red patches in her neck betrayed the fact that Hetty Schutter, principal and sometimes eighth-grade teacher, was getting a bit hot under the collar.

Huddled on the stage, seven little shepherds were in a visible state of befuddlement. Where a flock of angels was supposed to have come fluttering onto the stage, a mother had materialized, making unintelligible gestures. The shepherds stared at her sheepishly. The mother disappeared behind the curtain again. For a while nothing happened.

One shepherd had an itch and started vigorously scratching himself under his dusty old shepherd's robe. A second shepherd waved at his grandma. The third squirmed, pressing his knobby knees together because he was so nervous he had to pee. Something fell over behind the curtain with a crash. Then silence again.

The audience began stirring and grumbling. The fathers and mothers in the auditorium tried to maintain order, but that didn't stop scuffles from breaking out among brothers and sisters. Warnings were hissed that someone was going to get a spanking. Two folding chairs clattered to the floor.

At the side of the stage, the curtain billowed. Someone was looking for the opening, which was located three yards farther on, where the angels were supposed to have made their swooping entrance. Whoever was behind the curtain must have been driven by nerves rather than common sense, because it couldn't possibly have taken Charlie Chaplin, at his clumsiest, longer to finally make his entrance, all the way down to the far end of the stage where the curtain ended.

It was the headmistress.

"Uh... Ladies and gentlemen, children, due to circumstances beyond our control, our Christmas show has run into some difficulties we haven't quite been able to solve yet, and therefore..."

One of the shepherds behind her started crying.

"...we'll just resume selling tickets for our Christmas lottery, the proceeds of which..."

The weeping shepherd had wet his pants. A large dark spot was blooming on his blanket cape.

"...will pay for a new video projector for our school."

The principal hissed over her shoulder for a mother to come rescue the unfortunate shepherd, then went on: "The tickets cost one euro each, and you stand to win one of the lovely prizes donated by..."

A nervous mother mounting the stage from the side began by dragging off the wrong child, then led the right child in the wrong direction, to a door that wasn't a real door but rather a piece of scenery for the operetta club.

"...parents, friends, and our suppliers, for which we are ever so grateful. The ticket sellers will be coming through the auditorium during intermission. And uh..." She threw another quick glance over her shoulder. "And we'll have the intermission right now."

Her forehead was spangled with sweat. Turning around, she shooed the remaining shepherds past the bits of scenery meant to represent a meadow, and back through the opening in the curtain, where a little group of children in costume and their parental helpers huddled among the uneven bars and other gym equipment, a wooden ox and donkey, and Joseph and the Virgin Mary. It smelled of pee.

2

"Evert will be here any moment, buster," I said to Bas, who was asleep on the windowsill. Bas is a fat old tom-cat who always twitches one ear when I talk to him, to show me he's still alive. Other than that, there's not much animation. Except if he hears the word *cookie*, upon which he hoists himself to his feet and waddles over to me, head cocked to the side, waiting for his cookie. Bas is probably the only feline in the Netherlands to put away a pound of shortbread every week. Normal cats don't eat cookies.

Bas doesn't move much, but he still smells pretty bad. I expect it has something to do with his diet. I'm the only one who isn't bothered by his stench.

"Enjoy basking in here in the warmth while you can, fatso, because once Evert gets here, I'm putting you out on the balcony."

I was looking forward to the arrival of my good friend Evert. Loudmouth, bullshit artist, heart of gold. There's always something for us to grumble about, and always plenty of laughs. And then, the same routine every week: cocktail, nuts, cheese, sausage, light meal, game of chess, cup of coffee, last one for the road, and a contented goodbye.

3

Half an Hour Earlier—At the Supermarket

An old man behind Evert kept ramming his cart into the backs of his legs. The Turkish lady whose turn it was hadn't pre-weighed her green beans at the vegetable counter.

"I no understand."

"Vegetable counter, register four."

A whining little boy grabbed his mother's arm, causing a jar of applesauce to fall and shatter.

"Can I borrow your store card? Mine's in the jacket of my other pock...uh, I mean the pocket of my other jacket," the woman in line ahead of him asked. Evert handed her his card.

"Then you should think about keeping it in your...Oh never mind, just keep it," he grumbled.

Things just weren't going Evert's way. Hendrik had forgotten to stock up on peanuts and had called to ask if Evert could stop by the supermarket, because what's chess night without peanuts? Evert had thrown in two cans of beer as well, because he thought a shopping basket with only a bag of peanuts in it looked a bit sad.

And now he'd been standing on line at the checkout for nearly fifteen minutes to pay for those fucking nuts. Whenever life handed him lemons, Evert always got thirsty. As soon as he'd paid, he cracked open one of the cans, said "Cheers" to the cashier, took a swig, and went outside. There he unlocked his bike, took another gulp, and got on. The beer was lukewarm.

You don't usually see someone on a bike drinking beer. *It's probably illegal. Possibly because it means you can't put out your hand to signal you're stopping,* Evert thought to himself. He wondered if anyone had ever been ticketed in the Netherlands for failing to make the stop-signal. He'd been taught the stop-signal over sixty years before, in grade school: You put out your right arm and flap it up and down like a lame bird.

"What about hand brakes, then?" he muttered to himself. "If you had hand brakes, that stupid stop-signal would stop you from stopping."

He let out a belch.

At least Hendrik would be happy; he was bringing the peanuts.

His bicycle creaked and squeaked.

The steady rain slowly soaked him to the skin.

4

It was bedlam. Parents were trying to muscle their way back-stage via the only exit, while the head of school was pushing the lottery vendors against the tide into the auditorium. Meanwhile the grandparents and grandkids were thronging around the snack bar erected for the occasion. The mothers in charge of the lemonade, chocolate milk, coffee, and tea hadn't counted on the intermission being called this early and they were in such a hurry to fill the plastic cups that a great deal was spilled. Rivulets of coffee and lemonade dribbled onto the floor.

The teachers made half-hearted attempts to call for order, managing only to intensify the pandemonium. Meanwhile the school custodian was busy making sure, even in these difficult circumstances, that no one was chewing gum.

★ ★ ★

The gym wasn't exactly the best venue for theatrical performances. A couple of dad-volunteers had plastered the tall windows with red crepe paper, which made the gym look less like Christmas and more like a huge brothel. Although in a brothel you don't usually find wall racks, gymnastic rings, and 150 folding chairs. Red and white honeycomb-crepe Christmas bells and a puny Christmas tree were the only things that projected the "special mood of the feast of light." The custodian adamantly refused to put up a bigger tree, because, said Harry, "Who's going to clean up all those needles afterwards? And I don't have enough Christmas tree lights anyway." Good man, saving the school at least a handful of pocket change.

He was a thrifty man, Harry van Staveren, head custodian. He had a special line on cookies a few days past their sell-by date. He didn't see the need for having one teabag for every cup. The canteen was his bailiwick, and every dime counted. As steward of the first aid kit, he took pains to cut the Band-Aids into strips so skimpy that they wouldn't cover a chafed knee. "A penny saved is a penny earned," he'd preach if anyone ventured a timid objection. For all that, he was as lazy as a lion in the zoo. Somebody had made the mistake twenty-three years ago of giving him a permanent sinecure. "So," said Harry, "good luck to anyone who tries to get rid of me before my sixty-fifth birthday."

★ ★ ★

The custodian was standing at the bottom of the stage steps, the headmistress at the top.

"Something horrible has happened. It's, uh . . . awful, terrible, the shit's hit the fan!" she stammered. She was obviously not herself. Normally she'd never say "The shit's hit the fan." Normally she'd say something like "We've just had a little hiccup."

Come on, lady, just come out with it, he thought to himself. "Calm down, Hetty, first tell me what's happened, then maybe I can find someone to fix the problem."

She took a deep breath. "Harry, little baby Jesus has disappeared."

5

4:40 p.m.—Hendrik's Apartment

To: The Board of Amsterdam Football Club Ajax

Sirs,

This past Saturday's newspaper apprised me of the Ajax Board's proposal to issue a total ban on alcohol at the Johan Cruijff Arena, in response to disturbances by drunken soccer fans at the end of the Ajax–FC Utrecht match of 17 November last.

Your governing body wants to make teetotalers of fifteen thousand people because your security guards, together with the police, have for years been unable to keep about a hundred rowdy hooligans in check, most of whom are known by name and can be easily pointed out in countless video recordings.

A few questions:

1. Does the alcohol ban apply in the boardroom and skyboxes as well?

2. Has it not occurred to you, as it has to me, that the gents who wreck stadiums, hurl metal objects, and kick the living daylights out of people may perhaps not take your alcohol ban all that seriously?

3. What would you think if the town council, in reaction to a car parked illegally on your street, decided to impose a total parking ban on your borough?

Two further suggestions for our board's distinguished blockheads:

1. A decree making it illegal for old ladies, little kids, and young women to venture outside, so as to get rid of purse-snatchers, child molesters, and serial rapists for good.

2. Seeing that an enormous dog turd has just been left outside my front door, I think a nationwide ban on dog walking wouldn't be a bad idea. From now on, dogs are to relieve themselves indoors only.

I wish you wisdom, dear Ajax gentlemen, a great deal of wisdom, because that is what's lacking.

In conclusion I would like you to know this letter has also been sent to Letters to the Editor at the *Parool* newspaper.

Yours most sincerely,
H.G. Groen

There, that one can go in the mailbox, I said to myself. *I've fulfilled my social responsibility. Enough for today.*

"What's keeping Evert?" I asked myself out loud. "And did I remember to put the Jenever on ice?"

6

Five Minutes Earlier—Princess Margriet School

"The little baby Jesus is gone. We've looked everywhere. Gone. What's a Nativity play without a baby Jesus? For once we manage to wangle a real baby for the part, and now this!"

"Can't we just use a doll instead for now?" Harry suggested.

"The parents are in the auditorium, so we can't, they'd notice right away. You'll have to go tell them—the parents. God, they're already staring in our direction. Don't look, you idiot!"

Harry blanched. "Why me? I don't know those people. They're friends of Esther's. Can't she be the one to tell them? I'll go look for her."

"Easier said than done. Esther's out of town," Hetty snapped at him.

Harry was growing more and more agitated. "Yes, but you're always much better than I am at that sort of thing, and I've got to keep an eye on things back here."

"Harry, I have my hands full too."

"With what, then?"

"With loads of things to do, of course."

"So tell me, what things?"

"Listen, Harry, either you go tell those parents right now, or I'll have some things to tell about *you* to anyone who'll listen."

He broke into a sweat. "Okay, I'll call them aside—"

"That's right, you're going to call them aside and then you're going to tell them we've looked for their baby everywhere, but we have no idea what's become of their little boy. Or was it a little girl—the baby Jesus? Anyway, it's gone missing."

"In front of everybody?"

"No, of course not, take them to my office."

"And where was the baby seen last?"

"In the bathroom vestibule. It was quieter there, and the baby carriage was less in the way. I seem to remember it was you yourself who told Tjeerd to leave the carriage there. I'm going to go call the police." She disappeared through the curtains.

Harry made his way through the crowd toward a nondescript couple in the center of the auditorium who'd been staring at them all that time. The woman had taken pains, though not all that successfully, to make herself look festive: brown dress adorned with a brooch, a pair of sensible shoes below, and a pale face and limp hair above. The man appeared to have come straight from work, probably at an administrative office or something.

You could read the terrified premonition in their eyes from a distance.

"Ah, Mr. and Mrs. uh...Would you, uh...come with me please?" Harry was doing his best to appear calm and composed, but his voice cracked.

"What's going on? Is it Sabine? Is there something wrong with our baby?" Panic in the mother's eyes.

The father cleared his throat. "Is everything okay back there?"

"Oh yes, of course, there's just something we have to check on. Come with me, won't you?" The custodian couldn't come up with anything better to say. He was desperately trying to think of a way of getting out of this unscathed, but he couldn't see how to. He led the couple back through the pushing and shoving crowd to the steps on the side of the stage, clambered up the five steps, and steered the anxious parents past three mother-helpers having an animated conversation behind the curtain. They fell silent as the father and mother sidled past.

7

Evert rode his squeaking bike through the drenched city. The road was already getting dark and very busy. He made a left turn, tried to increase his speed, heard a dull crunch down by his bike chain, and suddenly his feet were pumping air. He swerved to the right, swiped the edge of the sidewalk, heard his beer skitter away along the pavement, and was only just able to avoid finding himself sprawled on his back on the sidewalk. "What next?" he said to himself. "Now my chain's come off too, damn it all."

"Watch where you're going, gramps," said a chubby blonde lady in bulging leggings.

"Oh, please excuse me, lard-ass," Evert said affably. That gave her pause. She wasn't sure if she'd heard correctly, hesitated, then gave him the finger just to be on the safe side and walked on.

He stared at his bike. There was the old-fashioned chain guard, rusted and gummed up with dirt. Somewhere within, a sagging chain dangled free of the chain wheel. He could try, against his better judgment, to pry off the guard, loop the chain back on, and prod those pieces back where they more or less belonged. Chances of success were close to nil. And even if it did work, it was more than likely that he'd have to do it all over again two blocks on. Hands smeared with grease, clothes smudged with grease, lots of cursing, ranting, and raving, finally resulting in having to walk the rest of the way anyway. Best just to concede defeat and accept it. He leaned his bike against the fence of a school building and locked it.

To make matters worse, he suddenly had to pee—bad. Evert looked around, panicked. The schoolyard was full of parked bicycles but was otherwise deserted. There must have been something going on inside. The front door had been left invitingly open, and schools, he reasoned, have toilets. He stepped into the empty hall and heard a distant buzz of voices. He pushed open a door at random. He saw a vestibule with four doors, three of which had a picture of a toilet on them. He dove into the first toilet with a sigh of relief, shrugged off his coat, and let it fall to the floor. His cold fingers couldn't get a good grip on the zipper of his fly. Time was of the essence. "I'd better not piss in my pants on top of everything," he muttered to himself.

A piece of fabric had gotten caught in the zipper, which was now stuck halfway. In a cold sweat and with a great deal of difficulty he yanked his pants down, plopping down on the little child-size toilet with a profound sigh just in the nick of time. "Ah, oh, what a relief it is," he muttered a few seconds later. But the happiness was of short duration. "Oh shit, my coat!" The toilet was too small, or he was too big for it. He had been in such a frenzy he hadn't realized he'd wet his coat that he'd dropped on the floor in front of him. "Shit, now this! Will my bad luck ever stop?" Cursing under his breath, he looked around for a towel or something else to use to dry his coat.

He jumped when he heard one of the doors in the little hall open.

Evert suddenly realized that you could see under the toilet doors. Spooked, he grabbed his wet coat and pulled his legs up off the floor as high as he could manage. In ten seconds his legs started to feel like lead; in twenty seconds he knew he wouldn't last another three seconds; but it took only twenty-two seconds for the door to close again. Relieved, he lowered his scrawny white legs back down to the floor.

But what to do about his coat? Cautiously he stuck his head around the toilet door. His mouth fell open in surprise: There was a baby carriage parked in the little hall; inside it a baby lay sleeping, and draped over the pram's handlebar was a long tan raincoat.

8

Harry van Staveren, head custodian, led the ashen-faced father and mother into the principal's office. Carefully he shut the door.

"Please, take a seat. Can I get you a cup of coffee?"

"Well, first I'd like to know what's going on," said the father.

Harry hesitated, swallowed, and, avoiding his gaze, mumbled, "Uh... eh, your child is missing."

"How do you mean?" asked the father foolishly.

The mother grew even smaller and paler than she already was and started to cry. "How's that possible, missing?"

"Yeah, how could our daughter just go missing? Wasn't anyone watching her?"

"Well yes, well yes, there was someone with her at all times, except for... uh... maybe just for a very short time." Harry couldn't think of any other way of saying it. "And I'm sure we'll find your baby very soon. She can't be far, I shouldn't think. Can I get you a cup of coffee in the meantime?"

All the mother was capable of was blubbering. There was panic in the father's eyes. "Where was she last seen?" he cried. "Who saw her last?"

"We still have to figure that out." Harry was sweating like a pig. "I'll just go and inquire for you if anything's come up yet. Please wait here." And without looking back he slipped out of the office in search of something or someone to hide behind as efficiently as possible.

The parents were stumped for a moment. Then the father dashed after the custodian, with the weeping mother on his heels. Blinded by her tears, she failed to see the swinging door, and it slammed in her face. She tottered. Her husband heard the clap, turned, hesitated, was first inclined to keep going, but then went back, grabbed his wife by the hand, and by the time he'd turned to resume his pursuit, the custodian had vanished from view.

"Where did he *go*?" People in distress tend to grab on to the first thing that's at hand, and in this case that was the custodian. The fact that he had now given them the slip intensified their distress.

"Coming through … excuse me … coming through please … sorry … coming through." In their own polite way, they barged through crowds of people and gymnastics equipment. A lady was jostled and had hot coffee spilled on her Christmas dress. "Whoa! Shit! Can't you look where you're going?" The veneer of civilization is often quite thin. Too thin for hot coffee spilled all over one's dress. The baby's mother didn't notice; she just kept stumbling after her husband. The father stepped into a corridor where he found at least one straw to clutch at. Through the window of a small room crammed with filing cabinets, boxes, and reams of paper, he spied the headmistress yelling at someone. A giant of a man, meek as a whipped dog. She could be heard raging at the guy through the closed door: "You nincompoop, you don't leave a baby buggy in a toilet unsupervised, who does that? When was it, when did you last check on it, when did you last see it? Say something, man!"

The nincompoop in question stammered, "Ha...uh... half an hour ago...or something...maybe twenty minutes." White threads of spit spanned the corners of his mouth. Drops of sweat rolled down his fat cheeks, and his eyes bulged out of their sockets. Everything about him signaled that he wished he could squeeze all of his 255 pounds down the drain and just disappear. "I was called away by Harry, he said I should start pouring the lemonade."

"If I tell you to watch some—" She broke off abruptly as she saw the baby's parents storming up to her. There was a moment of hesitation, then she assumed a friendly expression and opened the door.

"Oh please, do come in. I was just asking my colleague how things stand exactly," she said, pumping the parents' hands with an excessive shake, as if that would help to reassure them. "As far as I know, the little one has now been missing for ten minutes or so, but I'm sure we'll find her again very shortly. She can't be far. Please don't worry, maybe someone—"

"Of course we're worried! Extremely worried, in fact. Wha— What can we do now? People are out looking for her, aren't they? Where have they searched so far?" the father broke in.

"Everywhere, of course..." It occurred to the principal

just a bit too late that that wasn't a very reassuring answer, so she went on: "Just to play it safe, we might think of calling the police, just in case—you know."

"Just in case of *what?*" the ashen mother piped up for the first time.

9

Evert carefully emptied his pockets. Debit card, a pencil, a small pack of rolling tobacco, keys, a handkerchief, a rubber band, and a lighter. He spread the stuff out on the floor beside him. Next he considered what to do about his smelly, urine-soaked coat. It wasn't much good now; not worth taking home. He didn't see a trashcan, so he stuffed it in the toilet and shut the lid. Then, cautiously, he poked his head around the door to make sure the coast was clear, grabbed the clean coat hanging on the buggy, and shut himself back in the child-toilet cubicle. Maneuvering clumsily in the tight confines, he managed to get into it. It was a bit big for him, but it would do. He stuffed his belongings into the pockets and stepped out into the little hall.

In the center of the vestibule stood the baby carriage. He peered inside. A little pink hat and a tiny balled fist were the only things not buried beneath the blanket. He pulled down the blanket an inch or two. Two little eyes, shut, and a little nose made their appearance. God, what a small nose, thought

Evert, and such tiny nostrils! A miracle anyone could breathe through those!

He stood there gazing tenderly at the baby for a while. Then he shook himself. It was time to get out of there. The pram was blocking his way to the door, so he carefully rolled it back a few inches. Again he looked inside. The baby couldn't be more than a couple of months old, he guessed. The door to the corridor suddenly swung open; it almost gave him a heart attack. A little boy of around five stepped inside, clutching his daddy's hand. The father scowled at Evert suspiciously. The tyke asked, "Are you that baby's daddy?"

Evert hesitated a fraction of a second, then, bending down to the little boy's level, said, "No, I'm the baby's grandpa. Could you please hold the door open for me, so that the carriage can come through?" The little boy obediently held the door open. He pushed the carriage out into the corridor and turned around.

"Mind you don't use that first toilet, it's clogged."

Then he kept walking toward the exit. He did not hear the door to the toilet vestibule fall shut behind him but he didn't dare look back. Rocking the buggy across the outer threshold, he bumped it very carefully down the four front steps.

A woman on her way inside, in a beige raincoat and transparent plastic rain bonnet protecting her Christmas hairdo, gaped at him in surprise. "There's nothing in there, don't worry," he reassured her. She tried to get a peek of whatever was in the buggy, but Evert whipped it around, striding across the schoolyard toward the gate. There he turned right and then swerved into the first street on the left, to ditch anyone who might be watching him go.

He found himself on Purmer Promenade. The "Promenade" designation was meant to convey the street's allure, but that was only wishful thinking. After all, doesn't every main street in every village and every town nowadays present the same dreary landscape of Rite Aids and Starbucks, Marshalls and Goodwills? Anything that was once attractive or distinctive in those high streets has disappeared. King Mediocrity and Queen Monotony now ruled the roost with iron fists. Even the twinkling Christmas lights couldn't lift the gloom.

Look at me, trudging through the rain with a baby carriage and a real-life baby in it, Evert thought to himself. He leaned forward. "Let's just call you baby Jesus for convenience sake, shall we, seeing as it's nearly Christmas?" he said softly. "And then I'll be Joseph. Only, Mary is nowhere in sight. But don't worry, little Jesus, we'll be fine without her."

Only then did he remember where he'd been going when his bicycle chain came off. He was supposed to be at his friend Hendrik's for their weekly chess game, plus the snacking and the boozing. He couldn't help chuckling to himself. Wouldn't Hendrik be surprised to see Evert bearing a Christmas gift in the form of the little baby Jesus himself!

10

"Do you have any enemies, that you know of?"

As is the case in all professions, only a small percentage of police officers truly understand their jobs; most of them are just so-so, and a few are so short on talent that they should really be assigned to Parks and Recreation. The two officers who had been sent to investigate the missing baby appeared to belong to this last category.

"Do you have any enemies, that you know of?" the young cop, who couldn't be much older than twenty, asked the missing baby's bewildered parents a second time. They shook their heads in unison.

"Do you know if your baby could have been kidnapped, you know, for a ransom?" his colleague said, adding insult to injury.

The headmistress, unable to take any more of this, drew the two officers aside. "I don't wish to butt in, gentlemen, but aren't you jumping the gun just a little bit? Don't you want to arrange a search first? It may be a good idea to report back to headquarters too. Take a description of the missing person. Put out an APB and such. Try giving the parents some reassurance. Get started questioning people here and there. Ask for backup. That sort of thing."

The snarky tone went completely over the officers' heads. The first, a skinny youth with a tuft of goatee dangling from his chin, started explaining to the parents that most missing children wind up being found, while the other, short and stout, spoke into his walkie-talkie, asking for backup.

The mother began to cry again. Tears rolled down her cheeks, snot came out of her nose; mouth and chin trembled in utter devastation. The father clumsily tried to console her while giving the officer a description of the baby. "Yes, uh...small, about twenty-four inches, twelve weeks old, some black hair...uh, well, what does a baby look like, don't you know what babies look like?"

"What's the baby's name?" asked the heavyset officer, as if he'd just had a terrific new idea.

"Sabine," the mother sobbed.

"It might be more useful to find out what kind of baby carriage it was, and what clothes she had on," the principal snapped, just about ready by now to blow her top.

"All in good time, lady," said the goatee calmly, as if he had everything perfectly under control, "first the baby's last name."

"How does that matter? Are you going to ask every baby you see to introduce itself?" The father, too, was starting to understand that these guys weren't the brightest light bulbs in the box.

"What does the baby carriage look like?" the officer asked with some reluctance.

"A bit...uh, a beige buggy, the old-fashioned kind, with big wheels. And Sabine is wearing...Maartje, what does Sabine have on?" Maartje, however, wasn't in any state to give an answer. She was bawling her eyes out, using the sleeve of her shirt for a hanky. "I think something pink...Yes, I believe she was wearing something pink," said the father.

"That won't get us very far, sir," the stout officer informed him. "Practically all girl-babies are dressed in pink."

"Then don't ask the question if you already know the answer," the principal interjected, "and just go look for her! And I insist you get your chief of police involved."

11

Twenty Minutes Earlier—Bicycle Tunnel

Evert was sheltering just inside a bicycle underpass, staring at the dripping town park. He didn't have that far to go, but the rain was now coming down hard. It was just a few minutes' walk, tops, to the building Hendrik had recently moved into. The flat would be toasty and the Jenever nice and cold. Under normal circumstances he wouldn't have taken cover, no matter how hard it rained, but now he had a precious cargo to think of. He leaned over to peek under the hood. Ever since he and baby Jesus had set out together, it hadn't given a peep. The only things poking out from the blanket were still: one little fist, a little nose, and a couple of inches of face. The blanket was already getting pretty wet.

It wasn't the kind of buggy meant for long walks in the rain. More the kind meant for the trunk of a Volvo station wagon, Evert decided, the kind that snapped open, one-two-three, for a sprint from the parked car into the townhouse. If he kept going in this downpour, the buggy would soon become a bathtub. "I did read somewhere that infants are able to swim from birth, but I wouldn't want to take the chance..." he muttered. "And besides, I think you'd have to be an advanced swimmer to manage it with your clothes on." Evert was normally a man of few words, but he was making an exception for this occasion.

A bicycle was approaching. Evert hesitated. What would be the most inconspicuous way to act? What was an elderly man doing with a baby carriage in a bicycle tunnel? He couldn't think of anything except to continue peering inside the pram. The bicyclist rode past looking neither left nor right. It wasn't as if there was much to see anyway, since it was getting dark and the local juvenile demolition squad had busted all but two of the tunnel's ceiling lamps.

Evert was still hesitant. He'd been there for several minutes, and it didn't look as if the rain would stop any time soon. He couldn't stay there much longer with the baby carriage, because it was also getting damn cold. He'd just have to bite the bullet. He took off his newly acquired raincoat and spread it as a tent over the carriage hood. He knotted the sleeves as well as he could around the frame. Then he closed the top buttons of his shabby suit jacket, flipped up the collar, and stepped out into the pouring rain.

He walked as fast as he could, a bit hunched over, head bowed. Pushing the carriage with one hand, he used the other to keep the raincoat in place. Rain was pouring down his neck and along his back. His shoes were soon filled with water too, because the street was a mess of puddles. Evert had too much on his plate to try to avoid puddles on top of everything else. It occurred to him that he probably made a strange sight, but this wasn't the time to worry about it. The people cycling by were hunched deep inside their ponchos or rain slickers—clothing that doesn't make it easy to glance sideways, because all you see is the inside of your hood.

Evert was panting. Not far now. He could already see Hendrik's building.

A minute later found him clumsily attempting to hold open the entry door of Hendrik's building for both himself and the carriage to squeeze through. He did bump the carriage into the doorjamb, but—thank God—there was still no sound coming from beneath the raincoat. He rang the bell of number 227. The intercom crackled. "Evert Duiker, I presume?"

"Yes, plus a mystery guest, your honor," Evert replied. "And now open the fucking door, Hendrik, because we're perishing of the freezing cold here." There was a buzz, and Evert pushed open the second door leading to the elevator hall. The elevator door promptly slid open when he pushed the button. He stepped inside with the buggy and pressed the button for the seventh floor. Staring in the elevator's big mirror, he couldn't help chuckling to himself, even though he was frozen and soaked to the bone. "You won't believe your eyes, Hendrik, you old coot."

★ ★ ★

The elevator door slid open. Standing in the opening, hand outstretched, was Hendrik Groen. "A very good day, my dear fri—" His mouth fell open. "What do you have there, Evert, for God's sake?"

"Well, 'for God's sake' is well put in this case, Henkie, because for this special occasion I have brought you a little gift in the form of the baby Jesus himself."

"How did you get your hands on a *baby*, for God's sake?" Astonishment was written all over Hendrik's face.

"There you go again with 'for God's sake'! But yes, it is indeed a gift from the heavens, which has more or less landed in my lap. What I'm supposed to do with it I haven't the foggiest, man. We can't keep it, of course, since I've got to return it, but I thought it would be fun, just for one evening: two old men and a baby. Great title for a movie, by the way."

12

Harry the school custodian was seeing red. "They've left the entire shit show for me to clean up, of course," he seethed.

The gym was an unholy mess. The evacuation had been less orderly than the one laid out in the school's evacuation plan.

Shortly after the emergency intermission was called, the headmistress had sent the school's one and only male teacher into the gym, charged with getting everyone to leave the building as quickly and as quietly as possible. The man had made a brave attempt at radiating authority, but no dice. Nobody (including the man himself) understood why the Christmas pageant was suddenly being cut short. That was because the headmistress had decided to let as few people as possible know the reason for the show's abrupt cancellation, in the hope that the missing baby would suddenly reappear.

The teacher had grabbed the mic and stammered something about a sick lead actor but hadn't counted on a member of the audience asking who that was. When that did happen, the teacher, after some dithering, had taken a guess that it was the Virgin Mary, but Mary was standing six feet away from him sipping her chocolate milk. When Mary's father pointed that fact out to him, he'd stammered he "might" have been mistaken. "I'll try to sort it out directly, but right now it really would be best if you'd gather up your belongings and go home. Then we'll inform you as soon as possible what exactly was the matter. So now, if you'll excuse me . . . I have some things to see to back there, and I'll leave you in Mr. van Staveren's capable hands." And poof, he was gone.

Harry had started driving everyone toward the exit, but he encountered some defiant resistance. The children and their parents had coats and bags lying all over the place and weren't prepared to leave without their belongings. It was chaos.

Finally the gym was empty. The custodian, fuming, glared at the wreckage of overturned chairs, half-empty plastic cups, and crushed potato chips. He was just kicking a folding chair aside in a rage when the policeman with the goatee came in.

"I'd like to ask you a few questions," said the officer.

"Now? Do you have to?" said Harry with obvious reluctance.

"Yes, now."

"Well then go ahead, I suppose. I'll get home even later, oh well."

"You are the school caretaker?"

Harry nodded wearily.

"Could you tell me when you saw the child last?"

"Well, uh . . . actually . . . I never actually saw it, the baby," he suddenly said triumphantly. "All I ever saw was the baby carriage. I didn't look to see if there was anything inside."

"Let's assume the baby was inside the carriage; when did you see the carriage last?"

"Uh...let's see...I think...the last time I saw it, Tjeerd was standing next to it. He was supposed to watch it, I think."

"Who is Tjeerd?"

"That's our workfare guy, or whatever it's called these days. He was supposed to watch the baby. I guess he didn't do a very good job."

"You mean Mr. van Dongen? Mr. van Dongen has told my colleague that you told him to come help out in the auditorium," said the officer, in a tone betraying his fondness for TV's *Law & Order*.

Harry felt himself blush. "Well, if he told you that, it must be so, but I was here all by myself, and Hetty told me to fetch Tjeerd if I needed help."

"Who is Hetty?"

"The head—I mean, Mrs. Schutter."

"When you fetched Mr. van Dongen, did you notice what happened to the baby carriage?"

"Well, that was up to him, really. All I said was that he could just park the buggy in the john for the time being."

"In the what?"

"I told him to find a good place for it. Whatever he did with it is his responsibility. Am I right?"

"So you didn't see where he left the baby carriage?"

"I vaguely seem to remember he pushed it into the little hall where the toilets are. But it's still his responsibility, of course. It's got nothing to do with me. I mean, I had fifteen minutes to get two hundred glasses of lemonade and chocolate milk filled, so I wasn't really thinking about any babies. Should I have?"

It was quiet for a moment.

"Is there anyone who can confirm your story?" asked the officer.

"Well, let's see . . . Tjeerd was there of course, but knowing him, he'll probably come up with some self-righteous excuse. Other than that, I really didn't see anything, or anyone. No, not that I can remember."

"Nobody, then," said the officer pensively.

"Actually, I'd very much like to finish cleaning up this mess. Because if I don't do it now, I'll have to come in on my day off tomorrow. It's only three days to Christmas Eve, you see."

"I am sorry, but I can't have you touching anything. Everything has to stay exactly the way it is, for the crime scene investigation. And I must request that you remain here for the time being."

"So how long do I have to stay, then?" Harry sputtered.

"As long as necessary for the investigation. That's all for now." The officer tapped his cap in salute and disappeared in the direction of the headmistress's office.

Harry stared after him, cursing under his breath.

13

"Evert, Evert, Evert, what have you got us into now?" I knew my pal could sometimes be a bit impulsive, but this was especially ill-thought-out, even for him. A baby as a surprise Santa gift! I was finding it hard to hide my anger and irritation.

After untying the coat from the carriage, Evert hung it up on the coat rack and then rolled the buggy into the living room. We both leaned over the carriage. I pushed the little blanket down very carefully and removed the baby's drenched bonnet; the little one might catch a cold. Evert asked for a towel to dry himself off a bit and I handed him one. Then he flopped down on the sofa with a sigh.

"So? You'd better explain," I said sharply.

He looked chagrined. It was just starting to dawn on him that the presence of a baby carriage and baby in my apartment might be somewhat problematic.

"It was just an impulse, finding myself in that children's bathroom putting on someone else's coat, and peeking into that pram. It felt as if I'd been caught red-handed somehow."

"What children's bathroom, what are you talking about? You'd better start from the beginning."

"Well, uh…I was on my way here, but I suddenly had to pee very badly…" The whole story came tumbling out. He ended with: "And until I rang your bell, the whole thing seemed pretty funny to me. I must have had a blackout or something. What a bonehead I am."

"Sometimes," I agreed. My anger was giving way to pity.

I have known Evert for many years, but I don't think I'd ever seen him so crushed. I also know that there's not an ounce of evil in him. He is 100 percent trustworthy. If I had to go into hiding, it's to him I'd turn first. He wouldn't hesitate to find me a snug hiding place in a cellar, and they'd have to kill him first before he'd give me away.

"Okay," I said, "that was a pretty dumb move, but let's just leave it at that. We've got to get that baby back as soon as possible, because they must be going nuts trying to find it."

Evert nodded. He had nothing to say, another first.

"The parents must be out of their minds with worry," I added, rather unnecessarily.

"Yeah, damn it, Henk, I *know*. Let me think how to contain the damage a bit." He paused for a second. "I could just bring the thing back, but I don't think I can manage it without being noticed."

"It has to be done in secret, my boy. If you end up in the paper as the joker who kidnapped a baby just for fun, you'll never live it down. You're better off moving to the North Pole."

We were quiet for a while.

"And what if you went to the police and told them you'd found the pram unattended in the street?" I thought it wasn't a bad idea, all things considered.

No, that wasn't an option, said Evert, because he had run into a father and his little boy, and another woman, just outside the school.

I proposed returning the baby myself.

"Yeah, that makes you an accessory to the crime," Evert objected, "and then there'll be two old fools moving to the North Pole."

There was another silence. I suddenly realized my shoes were creaky, because I was pacing up and down. "What if," I suggested, "you took the baby somewhere close by, somewhere that's sheltered from the rain, and meanwhile I called the school and told them where to look for the carriage..."

"But why do you have to be the one to call?" Evert asked.

I explained the baby wouldn't have to be out in the cold for long that way. "And we've got to protect the pram with a plastic garbage bag or something, to stop it from getting even more wet."

"So then where's the best place for me to leave the pram?" my friend asked. After some deliberation, we decided on the bicycle tunnel underpass in the park. On further reflection, Evert didn't think I should call from my home phone. He thought they'd be able to trace the call, and so we decided I'd walk over to the phone booth at the bus station.

"If we leave at the same time, we'll be back at about the

same time too, ready to raise several glasses to a job well done." He was already back to his jovial self.

I looked up the number of the school in the phone book. Evert went over the plan as he put his coat on. "Okay, I'll take the carriage over to the bike tunnel. You'll start walking in the opposite direction. You'll get to the bus station in... let's say ten minutes or so, and there you'll call the school."

"All right, that's what we'll do. Let's synchronize our watches."

"Huh?"

"Never mind." I put my coat on. "I'll go downstairs first to make sure the coast is clear. When you hear me ring the buzzer, get in the elevator with the buggy as quick as you can, and then head straight for that tunnel. I'll already be on my way."

A few moments later I stepped into the elevator, descended seven floors, stuck my head out to make sure no one was coming, and then pressed my own buzzer. I heard the elevator go back up, let the entrance door fall shut behind me, and sauntered up the street without looking back.

14

"Would you like a coffee? Tea? A cold drink perhaps?" For the third time the mother shook her head. White as a sheet, she was sitting hunched and staring into space with tears rolling down her cheeks. The father sat next to her, just as pale.

The other people in the office were the headmistress, the workfare guy, the second- and fifth-grade teachers, and two newly arrived police officers. Spread throughout the building were six members of the detective task force searching for clues. The custodian had been told to follow them around in case they needed anything or had questions.

The two officers who'd been first on the scene were now keeping watch out in the schoolyard in the icy rain. They'd been relieved at their indoor posts by two sergeants with more stripes on their arms and more experience. There was a lot of phoning back and forth with top brass. A task force was being assembled for a manhunt in the immediate environs, which was to start as soon as possible.

The headmistress was busy composing a list of all the

children and parents who had been at the Christmas pageant. The list was being emailed to police headquarters, where four desk officers were about to start on a round of phone inquiries. The mayor and chief prosecutor had been informed, and if the baby wasn't located by seven o'clock, they would both go to the police station to direct the crisis task force in person. The press liaison officer was on his way. The first phone call from a local newspaper had already come in. "It won't be long," said one of the officers, "before we have twenty reporters and five camera crews on the doorstep."

The headmistress was sorry she had cancelled her hairdresser's appointment yesterday.

★ ★ ★

The police were dealing with their own problems. The force was short-staffed, and the call for reserve officers wasn't bearing fruit. For a thorough search of the environs, they'd need some thirty men, and right now they only had fifteen. "To conduct a house-to-house search with so few men won't work," sighed Police Captain De Rooy, who, as the highest-ranking officer, had temporarily taken the reins while awaiting further instructions from headquarters. It wouldn't be long before the chief of police himself got on the phone. *Maybe that's him*, De Rooy thought when the phone rang.

The headmistress picked up. "Princess Margriet School, Mrs. Schutter speaking." She listened a moment. Then, practically pulling the stripes off the closest policeman's uniform with her free hand, she started pointing and jabbing furiously at the receiver. "Excuse me, what did you say?... Let me repeat: the tunnel underpass in Juliana Park, beneath Paulus Potter Lane? And with whom am I—?" The other party had apparently already hung up. For a moment she was too flabbergasted to say anything. Then she returned to her senses. "I just had a call from a man who says the baby and the baby carriage have been left in a tunnel in Juliana Park, the underpass at Potter Lane."

"What did you say?" two officers said in unison.

The father almost fell out of his chair. The mother stood up, still weeping, but even louder now, with howling intakes of breath. As the father scrambled to his feet and threw an arm around his wife's shoulders, the captain snatched the phone out of the headmistress's hand, to see if anyone was still on the line. "Hello? Hello?" Then he took out his walkie-talkie and in his most portentous police voice said, "H.A. 23 speaking, all units to Juliana Park, all units to Juliana Park, the underpass at Poulter Lane. Baby carriage containing an infant supposedly left there. I repeat: Look for a baby carriage with infant, probably parked somewhere around the tunnel beneath Poulter Lane."

"Potter Lane," the headmistress corrected him.

"Correction, Potter Lane, the tunnel beneath Potter Lane, Potter, you know, as in Harry, the kid magician."

"No, it's named for Paulus, Paulus Potter," the headmistress interjected again, "the painter who painted bulls." It was the ingrained schoolmarm in her.

The officer glared at her, annoyed, and continued barking into his walkie-talkie. "H.A. 23 calling all units, detain any suspicious persons in the surrounding area and convey them to HQ. Over."

The mother of the missing Christmas baby was anxiously putting on her coat. The father was looking for his own coat, then realized he didn't have it and proceeded to button up his suit jacket instead.

"Where's that underpass, that bicycle tunnel?" the father asked one of the teachers, who shook her head and said she didn't know. "Does anyone here know where that tunnel is?" the father yelled, frantic.

"I think it would be more sensible if you waited here," said the officer, but he had underestimated parental instincts. There was finally something for them to do, and there was nothing even ten cops could do to stop them.

"Do you know where the Aldi is?" the workfare guy interjected. The father nodded. "From the Aldi you head toward the city center, and a few hundred yards on, to your left . . . no, on your right, you'll see the entrance to the park, and the tunnel's just beyond."

"Mind your own business, Tjeerd," the headmistress snapped at him.

"But I'm just telling them where to go."

"Mind your own business, Tjeerd," she said again, even more pointedly, and turning to the parents, "I do think it's best for you to wait here until . . ."

But they were already stumbling out the door and were no longer listening. The father got his jacket caught on the door handle, but he released himself with a firm tug and stepped out into the corridor.

15

I paced up and down near the door buzzer, anxious to let Evert in. He should have been back by now. Still, I jumped when the bell buzzed in my ear a minute later.

When the elevator door slid open, the first thing I saw was the baby carriage, with an ashen Evert behind it in the elevator's white fluorescent glare.

"What's happened, how come you've still got the baby?" I asked, dragging my friend as quick as I could back into the apartment and locking the door.

"There were all these teenagers hanging out there. At least ten of them. I hung back a few minutes when I saw them, but it didn't look as if they were leaving any time soon. And I didn't dare wait any longer. I didn't dare just leave the carriage there either, in the dark and in the rain. So I just came back. And by the time I got to your door, I could already hear the sirens."

"Well, now those poor kids are having a visit from the cops, I imagine. Won't they be surprised. Both sides, in fact.

The cops are in for a shock too." In spite of our predicament, I couldn't help sniggering. "It's going to be fun and games tonight."

We sat there for a while staring into space. Evert poured himself a drink. I uncorked a bottle of red wine. It had one of those newfangled plastic corks. "So it isn't a cork, really, because a *cork* is made of *cork*," I mused, "so you can't really un-*cork* this kind of bottle, you un-*plug* it. And then, most often, you can't plug the plastic cork back into the bottle, and if you *do* manage to wring it in, you have to use the corkscrew to wrench it out again, because it's so stuck you can't pull it out by hand. Modern crap. Just give it a screw top and call it a day."

"What are you gassing on about, Henkie? Trying to come up with some new ploy?"

"No I was thinking about something else, actually, about those newfangled plastic corks that . . ."

We both froze. From the carriage came a loud wail.

16

Siren wailing, the cop car came tearing along the bike path and down into the tunnel. A gang of ten or so juveniles, aged sixteen or seventeen, were caught in the headlights. Blindsided. They began to yell.

"We didn't do anything, man! They can't accuse us of anything. Just stand your ground." And they did stand their ground, although most of them tried shrinking to the back of the pack.

The cruiser screeched to a halt. Two cops jumped out, then gazed around, bewildered. They seemed to be looking for something else.

"Did any of you see a baby carriage down here?"

It didn't immediately occur to most of the boys that this was a strange thing to ask, in that spot and at that time of day. One of them did find it funny, and he started mimicking a baby crying.

The mood immediately turned hostile. A second cruiser drove up, tires squealing. Two more cops jumped out.

One of the boys decided it was time to get out of there and he took off to the far end of the tunnel. A second one decided to follow his example. They were out of luck, however, because yet another cop car was just pulling up on that side. The officers instinctively reacted to the running boys the way hunting dogs react to a fleeing rabbit.

"*Freeze!*" In the middle of the bike tunnel stood an officer just a few years older than the runaway kids. There was a din of yells, and one of the two boys stopped short. The other kept running.

"Halt!" came another warning from two different directions. As the teens realized they were trapped, all was quiet for a moment. Even the boy trying to run away stopped dead in his tracks.

"Up against the wall, against the wall! Now! All of you."

"Why? We ain't done nothing wrong. We were just standing here!"

"Shut up and get up against the wall, NOW!"

"I was just standing here minding my own business!"

"Turn around. Hands against the wall."

In the glare of headlights from three cruisers, the tunnel now held a row of boys neatly lined up with their hands against the wall.

One of the cops picked the boy who looked most scared out of the lineup, loomed over him, and demanded to know where the baby carriage was. The kid had no idea what he was talking about and looked at his friends nervously.

"Where's that baby buggy?" the officer asked again.

"I don't know. What you talkin' about, there's no baby carriage here, can't you see for yourself?"

"HQ, HQ, Cruiser 27 here. Negative on baby carriage in the bike tunnel. But we do have ten or so suspects. I think. Please instruct, over."

"HQ here, HQ here. Reinforcements on the way. Detain all and bring them in. Over."

"What about the baby carriage, what should we do about that? Over."

"As soon as there are enough of you, start combing the grounds. Over."

"How many is enough? Over."

"Just start with as many as you can spare from arresting those guys. And make it quick. Over."

"Copy. Over and out."

"Good luck. Over and out."

It was an unusual sight: six agitated officers and ten agitated youths in the beams of six headlights and three sets of flashing lights in a tunnel with smashed lamps and walls covered in colorful graffiti as well as aphorisms like "What's the plan Stan," "Jesus Rocks," and "Shirley is a fucking whore."

Drawn up in the middle of the bike path stood the boys' shiny scooters, seven of them all in a row. One of the officers took a step back and accidentally bumped into the nearest of them. With a great clatter four fell over, one after another, like dominos. Everyone looked around, startled. For a moment it was shockingly quiet. Then all hell broke loose.

The fattest and slowest cop was the first to be head-butted and slammed to the ground before he knew what was coming. The second one was kicked in the balls, and he doubled over. The third and fourth were able to more or less duck the blows, and they began backing away. Officers five and six had been standing at some distance, so they'd had time to pull out their batons and start swinging away to rescue their colleagues. But the cops were outnumbered, and there was no chance for them to regroup. Within a few seconds three cops were flat on the ground and the remaining three were backed up against the wall, warding off a posse of furious punching and kicking teenagers. One officer's baton was immediately kicked out of his hand, leading to a frantic struggle on the ground. A cacophony of screams and profanities ensued. Then, suddenly, the tables were turned on the battlefield. Two police vans came squealing up, and within a couple of minutes the situation looked very different. Ten boys were now lying smack on the ground, hands cuffed behind their backs.

One of the cops, sitting with his back against the wall, was nursing a bleeding nose. A few feet farther on, two others sat holding their heads in their hands, trying to figure out what had gone wrong.

In the tunnel entrance a man and a woman appeared, frozen and pale as ghosts: the distraught parents. Both drenched to the skin. The man wearing no overcoat, just his suit jacket.

"HQ, HQ, come in please. Cruiser 27 calling. Over."

"HQ speaking, go ahead. Over."

"Requesting an ambulance and make it quick, we have a couple of injuries. And enough vans to transport ten detainees. Over." And to the nearest police officer, he barked, "Tell those folks over there to move along."

"27, 27, what about the baby carriage? Over," his radio crackled almost simultaneously.

17

From the little balcony of my two-room flat I peered in the direction of the park. I spotted seven police cars, an ambulance, and a fair number of motorcycle police. A carnival of flashing lights in the dark. Unbelievable. Ever since I'd moved into this apartment on a temporary basis, over a year ago now, my life had grown considerably quieter than before. To the point of snoozing, I should add. To my mind, there was nothing wrong with a bit of excitement every once in a while, naturally, but *this* was really a bit over the top. I had somehow made myself an accessory to a baby's kidnapping and, in the park around the corner, launched a pitched battle over a baby carriage that wasn't even there. An hour ago my prime concern had been whether the Jenever was sufficiently chilled. Now my pal Evert was sitting in the living room with a baby on his lap that didn't seem to be in a mind to stop wailing any time soon. I went inside and shut the balcony door. Outside on the balcony, Bas stared at me reproachfully.

"Can't you take over from me for a bit, please, Henk?"

came a forlorn plea from the Naugahyde three-seater. "The screaming's getting on my nerves."

"The kid must simply be famished."

"Is there anything to eat?" Evert asked stupidly.

"Potato chips, liverwurst, cheese sticks, everything babies like to eat."

"Funny, ha ha."

"Yeah, seeing that you're such a genius, stealing a baby, I'd have expected you to bring along some sustenance for our young guest as well. What do you think about an infant Bloody Mary? I'll see if she'd like it extra spicy. At least, I think it's a she, anyway, on account of all the pink."

"If you'll just take a turn holding her for a bit, I'll make a quick run to the supermarket to see if I can find some baby food."

"You know what, pal? Why don't you stay here and let me go to the supermarket? I can't stand crying babies either."

"Oh okay, but please hurry." Evert was looking a bit the worse for wear.

"I'll be back as soon as I can."

I put on my coat, checked to see if I had my wallet, and walked out the door.

Outside it was still drizzling. A siren wailed: yet another ambulance. In the distance the flashing lights were clearly visible. I made a mental note to watch the news later.

I strode along at a good pace and reached the super-market in five minutes. Finally, here was my chance to take advantage of the new extended shopping times.

I knew my way pretty well around the bread and cheese aisles, but it had been a while since I'd had to find the baby food. Thirty-eight years or thereabouts. I had to stop and think for a minute.

A little later I found myself confronted with a shelf holding dozens of different Gerber baby food jars. How old might the baby be? Two months, four months, six months? Just to be on the safe side, I filled my basket with two jars for each age group. Only, it seemed that four months was the youngest category. In case the baby drank nothing but milk, I chose the smallest container of powdered formula for children zero to six months. A jar of pureed fruit wouldn't hurt either, I decided; I could always eat it myself. I was on my way to the checkout when it occurred to me that our Christmas baby probably hadn't been changed for hours. Diapers! And baby wipes. When I'd found those as well, I glanced in my basket. A rather unusual haul for a man in his seventies. Again I turned around; I had to find some other items to serve as cover. A can of soup, dish detergent, and a bottle of wine—those would do as a smokescreen, I figured. Still, at the checkout I had the feeling that people were casting curious glances at my basket.

"Forty-four euros and eighty-five cents, please."

"Boy, that's pretty steep."

"Excuse me?" the cashier asked.

"No, nothing. I was just talking to myself."

"Don't worry about it," she said, bored.

At least she didn't add "grandpa."

Once outside I gave a sigh of relief and walked back to my building as fast as I could. Some several hundred yards away, peace had not yet returned to the park. I could still see police car lights flashing, but I didn't have the time to worry about it. I had to get back to a friend in need.

18

He'd witnessed plenty of misery in his time, but this situation was leaving Officer Voorberg completely rattled. He'd taken off his police cap to wipe the sweat off his forehead with a large handkerchief. By some unlucky coincidence, the hanky was embroidered with *"Who's my daddy?"* It was a Father's Day present from his five-year-old little girl. He quickly put it away.

Across from him sat two of the most pathetic bundles of misery he'd ever had in his office: Johan and Maartje Verbeek, parents of Sabine Verbeek, aged twelve weeks and lost for two hours.

"Sir, ma'am…the situation as we gather it now is as follows. Your daughter was taken in her baby carriage between…" he glanced at his notes, "ten minutes past four and four twenty-five by an elderly gentleman in a beige rain-coat. Which may be your own raincoat, sir, which had been left draped over the carriage. We found another raincoat in one of the children's toilets, and we suspect it belongs to the perpetrator. The coat is being examined as we speak. Two witnesses saw this man leave the toilet vestibule with the carriage, headed in the direction of the exit. These two witnesses, a man and his five-year-old son, are being fetched from home in order for them to make a statement and give a description as far as they are able. We may be looking at a kidnapping. Can you think of any reason someone might want to kidnap your baby?"

The father shook his head slowly. "No, I can't for the life of me think why anyone would do that." The mother, who kept dabbing at her bloodshot eyes with a grubby handkerchief, just shook her head. She seemed too dazed to follow the conversation.

"Look," the officer went on, "the most puzzling thing is the phone call announcing your baby would be left in a tunnel inside the park. Well, I believe you saw with your own eyes what transpired there, but we haven't found the baby carriage. Perhaps the suspect was scared off, but it's also quite possible it was a deliberate diversion. Your child may have been taken for another reason."

"Such as?"

"Well, anything, really. The guy might want to keep her for himself, for instance."

A heartrending wail from the mother.

"You didn't notice anything unusual in the past...let's say, the past week?"

Again the father shook his head very slowly. "No." He glanced at his wife and saw it was pointless to ask her anything. "Don't you have anything to give my wife, to calm her down a bit?"

"We'll have a doctor take a look at her shortly."

"And so what are you going to do now?"

"Right now there's a search on in the school's environs, in the park around the bicycle tunnel as well as any other underpasses in the area. And we are questioning everyone who was present at the school. Provided we can round up enough police officers, we are going to commence a neighborhood-wide search this very evening, otherwise it'll have to wait until tomorrow morning. We have put a task force of some twenty-five officers on the case."

"Is that sufficient?" asked the father.

"Well, I can't really say. We're doing our best. And besides that, we're working on issuing an Amber Alert."

"Can't that be done immediately?"

"We're giving it a little more time. At this time there are still deliberations ongoing here at the station. The mayor is already here, and they're waiting for the arrival of the public prosecutor, the chief of police, and the press liaison officer. There'll probably be a short press conference later tonight, because we are already being hounded by the press."

"Do we have to attend?" the father asked. He kept rubbing his forehead.

"For now I think it's preferable that you go home and try to get some rest. Do you live far? Do you think you're capable of driving, in fact? Actually, no, just leave your car here, I'll have a colleague take you home. Would you like the doctor to have a look at your wife first? Two of our people will stay with you for the time being, but would you like a friend or family member to be there as well?"

That was too many questions at once. Ashen-faced and a total wreck, the father stared at him blankly. His wife's face was blocked from view by two trembling hands and a wadded handkerchief.

19

"Yeah, so what do we put it in?" asked Evert, holding the can of formula.

After some deliberation we had concluded the baby was still probably on the young side for solid baby food. We had tried stuffing some fruit puree into her with a teaspoon, but it had dribbled right out again.

"And the little darling just won't stop crying, although I must say it's rather restrained." I noticed I was starting to feel more and more tender-hearted toward the baby.

"What do we put it in, Hendrik?" Evert asked again, beatifically.

"How do I know, maybe a little cup or something."

"A little cup, says the man. Since *when* do babies drink from a cup? How about a bottle, with a nipple?"

"Yeah, of course, I know that, but we don't have one."

"No, we don't have one. Because you didn't *buy* one. So I'll just have to go out and get one, otherwise we'll never in a million years get anything down her little throat."

"But do they sell them at the convenience store?"

"I doubt it. I think I'll have to find a drugstore. Where's the closest pharmacy?"

"Uh . . . I think it's the one on Breugel Square, the BanDaid. If it's still open, that is."

"It's late-night shopping for Christmas; at least that's one thing going our way. The BanDaid . . . is it really called the BanDaid?"

"Yeah, funny name, isn't it?"

"Well, as long as they have bottles and nipples, they can call themselves SuckNipple, for all I care. Is there anything else you would like from the drugstore? Band-Aids? Ribbed condoms? Hemorrhoid cream?"

"Just hurry. I think she's very hungry."

Evert put on his new raincoat, but then had second thoughts. He took it off and a few seconds later was out the door in my brown winter coat.

* * *

Evert was waiting for the elevator when the door to the apartment next door swung open and a rosy-faced lady wearing just a touch too much makeup stepped into the hall in a dress that was a bit too young for her age, which she probably wore to show off her large bosom. Evert, never unmoved by big tits, stepped aside to let her into the elevator first. She was carrying a garbage bag.

"So, were you visiting Mr. Groen?" she asked with a mixture of suspicion and nosiness.

"No, I am *still* visiting Mr. Groen. I just have to run an errand for him."

"Well, I did hear the door open and shut again, and the elevator, so I thought to myself: *My neighbor must be having people over.*"

Evert didn't think it was farfetched to think she might have been standing at the door with her garbage bag at the ready the moment she heard her neighbor's front door open again. For a moment or two there was silence. Then she couldn't keep quiet any longer.

"I even thought I heard a baby crying, over at Mr. Groen's. Crazy, isn't it? On my part, I mean. Yup, if you're alone most of the time, you start imagining all sorts of crazy things."

"Yeah, that does happen."

"Actually, I don't even know if Mr. Groen has any kids, or grandkids. And here we've been living next door to each other for almost a year. Crazy, isn't it?"

"Yeah, it was different in the old days," said Evert, who was getting a bit flustered, not only by the woman's obvious snooping, but also by the décolleté that was swimming at him from all directions in the elevator's mirrors. He was glad when they came to a stop on the ground floor. "Have a nice evening," he said quickly, as she seemed about to resume her interrogation. She looked crestfallen. He heard her say, "You too," and saw her still standing in the elevator clutching her bag of garbage until the door slid shut again. He pushed Hendrik's buzzer; a few seconds later his friend's voice came through on the intercom.

"Put on some music and turn up the volume, pal, because

there's someone with huge knockers with her ear to the wall to see if she can hear a baby crying."

"What are you talking about now?"

"About your next-door neighbor."

"Oh, that one."

"See you."

Evert turned and hurried to the drugstore.

20

7:00 p.m.—Police Station

"We have two seemingly unconnected problems that are somehow linked. Problem number one: We have an abducted baby on our hands who was supposed to play the baby Jesus and whose disappearance will be splashed all over the world's headlines unless she turns up again very soon. And problem number two: We have to figure out what to do with the ten punks we arrested, who are all claiming they didn't do anything. And it may be true that they didn't really do anything, but that may be because we handcuffed them first. Juicy detail for the reporters who are about to descend on us in search of sensation. The dustup was a direct consequence of the search for the little girl Jesus in her baby carriage, and our officers, in their youthful zeal, made a couple of unnecessary arrests." The person speaking was Chief Prosecutor Stork. Just a half hour before he'd been at home with his wife solving a Sudoku puzzle. The Sudoku session, lubricated with a bottle of Rioja, was usually the prelude to a canoodling session on the sofa. Afterward they would order a takeout pizza. But now, instead of his wife's lovely ass, the chief prosecutor found himself face to face with the bloated visage of Chief of Police Graven, and inhaling the pungent scent worn by Mrs. Schaarsberg Donk, the mayor. He sighed.

"What's the situation now?" asked the mayor, who had been pulled from a reception at the town hall in her formal getup.

"Well, not great," said the chief of police, who was picking at his mustache as if grooming himself for lice. "We don't know much. The baby was left in a school bathroom for a short time before being abducted by an elderly man in a beige raincoat. It happened at four fifteen or thereabouts. At five thirty the school received a phone call that the baby carriage would be left in a bicycle tunnel in Juliana Park. There we encountered not a baby, but ten riled-up juveniles."

"Were they riled up from the start or were they riled up by the riled-up cops?" Stork wanted to know.

"Well, look, you're looking for a three-month-old baby, and instead you're confronted with a gang of unruly sixteen- or seventeen-year-olds, that's quite an adjustment to make for my men. And before they knew it, it turned into a great big brawl, with two men down."

"Two?" asked the mayor.

"Not counting the juveniles for convenience sake," Stork said sardonically.

"What's an old guy doing with a baby anyway?" the police chief wondered.

"And, more specifically: Where *is* the old guy with the baby, anyway?" Stork replied drily.

"A little less cynical please, Mathieu," the mayor

admonished. "For all that the predicament itself is most unfortunate, of course, this business also means a great deal of negative exposure for the city, once the press gets wind of it. And that requires damage control, not snark."

Oh blah-blah-blah, Mathieu Stork fumed to himself, thinking wistfully of the wine bottle on the table back home, and of his wife's lovely ass.

"Stork the Cork," the policeman offered innocently, "that's what they call you at the district office, did you know that?"

"An honorary moniker, Wiebe, I consider it a compliment," Stork replied.

"Gentlemen, please," the mayor intervened sharply, "a baby's been kidnapped and we can expect some blowback regarding our treatment of the teens in the park; therefore, I think it would be best to put personal antipathies aside and concentrate on what really matters. For instance: What measures are being taken right now?" She cocked her head at the police chief.

"Search of the environs, all attendees of the school's Christmas pageant are being questioned, and the men are out scouring the park. We're also trying to trace that phone call. It was probably made from a public phone, but we're not sure yet. Forensics is examining a raincoat that is presumed to be the kidnapper's, and they're combing the school's bathrooms for evidence."

"Okay, that's something we can report at the press conference anyway. What's keeping the city press officer anyway?"

"This is a job for the police press liaison," said Stork.

"Have him come too then, Wiebe. What time is the press conference scheduled for?"

"Ten o'clock. We still have a little time."

"What are we doing about those juveniles?"

"Keeping it as quiet as we can. We'll try to downplay it as much as possible, avoid any and all provocation, and we'll let them go as soon as we can with a summons for assault of police officers in uniform. We'll inflate the assault charges a bit, but not too much. Might as well throw in for good measure that they were hampering the police in the search for the kidnapped baby. I'll have my own press officer come too, then. Together with your guy they'll have to work up a draft for a press release ASAP, and run it by us."

The mayor nodded.

"Does anyone want coffee?" the chief asked. "And what's the baby's name, anyway?"

21

The school custodian peeked into the bathroom through a crack in the door. Three men in there were leaning over a small toilet. A detective wearing latex gloves was carefully fishing a dripping raincoat out of the bowl. A second one held open a plastic bag; the coat disappeared into it. Number three wrote the time and location of the discovery on a sticker.

"I'll just ask what we should do with this," said the one who seemed to be in charge, placing a call. "Hello, De Rooy here. We're still at the school, and we've just fished a raincoat out of a toilet, probably belonging to the guy who took the baby. The coat may hold clues to his identity or place of residence. May we go ahead and examine it right here, or should we send the evidence to the lab?"

There was a pause.

"To the lab? Fine."

The custodian gave a sigh of relief. That would probably save quite a bit of time.

One of the gumshoes kicked the door open, whacking Harry in the nose.

"Shit... what the...?" He rubbed his nose gingerly.

"Oh, sorry, I didn't know there was anyone standing behind the door."

"I wasn't standing there, I was just on my way inside. I really have to lock up the school now."

"This school is going to get locked up when I give permission to do so," the captain broke in, "but if you'd like to go home, I can't stop you. You are not a suspect. For now."

The head had given the custodian specific instructions not to leave the building until everyone was out, and he didn't dare disregard that order. "How long do you gentlemen think you'll still need, in order to finish up?" he asked humbly.

"Well, if everything goes well, we should be done here in a couple of hours. And I wouldn't say no to a cup of coffee."

The custodian slunk off to the coffee machine like a sulky dog with its tail between its legs. "My whole evening down the drain," he muttered.

Walking past the main entrance, he noticed several bright camera lights shining in. The reporters outside saw him and tapped on the window. Harry opened the door a crack. "Go home! There's no one around anymore. There's nothing to see either." He'd have done better to keep the door closed. To scare off the ladies and gentlemen of the press, you need something more impressive than a guy in a janitor's smock. A guy with a machinegun would be a more effective option, but even that wouldn't guarantee success. Two mics were instantly poked through the door opening, cameras were busy filming through the window glass, and Harry was bombarded with shouted questions. Reporters started pushing at the door from the other side.

Harry wasn't in any mood for that. He put his full weight against the door, which slammed shut, only with two arms caught between. There were screams and shouts. He let go for an instant, then immediately, with all his might, pushed the door shut, locked it, and made himself scarce.

"Fucking paparazzi!"

He made his way to the kitchenette, poured water into the coffee machine, took out a filter, frugally measured out the coffee scoops, and switched on the machine. He wondered if he could bill someone for those three cups, maybe even for six. As a matter of fact, it occurred to him that people were sometimes handsomely compensated for interviews nowadays.

"Too bad that Hetty would probably fire me if she saw my face on television," he muttered to himself. Couldn't he think of a way around that?

22

The wastepaper basket was already filling up nicely with empty beer cans. Two fat guys in their fifties sat at a Formica table, each with an Amstel and a stack of papers in front of him. They were staring dully at a small TV on a metal filing cabinet six feet away. The local news was reporting that a baby had been snatched from an elementary school. Pictures of a schoolyard and behind it, in the dark, the school building itself.

"Holy smokes," one of the men said. "That's my brother's school."

"Is you brother still at school, then?" asked the other.

"No, bonehead, he works there, he's the caretaker." He practically spat it out.

Wil van Staveren, "Staff" to his acquaintances (because he didn't have any real friends), worked for the sanitation department. He was getting in some overtime this evening; that way he could have a few beers on the boss's time, without having to deal with his nagging old lady.

Sitting across from him was Rinus Schepper. He wasn't in any hurry to get home either. Safe to say, his marriage wasn't what it used to be, either. It wasn't as bad as at the van Staverens', where Wil and his wife each rested their feet on a piece of threadbare carpeting beneath their respective armchairs, turned to face their own individual TV sets, which they listened to through separate headphones; that way there could be no bickering about which program to watch. Verbal communication was kept to a strict minimum, such as the fact that they were out of potato chips... Otherwise, in the evening they communicated largely by gesture. Both of their grown children were out of the house and didn't come home very often. They only showed up for birthdays, Christmas, and New Year's. "I'll celebrate Easter only if it doesn't fall on a weekend," was Wil's annual wisecrack. From May until October, they spent every weekend in the trailer in Bakkum, where they could enjoy watching TV in a completely different setting.

"That's *Mr.* Bonehead, to you," said Rinus after a long silence.

On the television a reporter was elaborating on the news that there was no news to elaborate on. Yes, a baby had gone missing. Probably kidnapped. It had all happened right here; he indicated the school's front door behind him.

"Not such a dumb move, actually, kidnapping a baby," said Wil. "At least a baby can't run away."

"And it can't identify its kidnappers, so it can't give the police a description afterward either," Rinus added.

"I'll give my brother a call tonight. To see what he knows

about it." Wil burped and stared off in the distance, lost in thought.

Rinus looked up at the clock and began sliding the papers in front of him into a folder. "Nice work, Staff," he chuckled. "We'll need at least two more evenings next week, I should think, to get through this paperwork. I'll tell Hooier tomorrow that we got a lot done and we'll have the backlog straightened out before the end of the year. You hear me, Staff?"

Wil looked up and nodded, swigged the last dregs of beer, tossed the empty can with a well-aimed shot into the waste basket ten feet away, and burped again. He decided to call his brother as soon as he got home.

23

I sat down with a deep sigh. This was the strangest day I'd had in years.

"We've got to set the alarm, Evert."

"Why?"

"Well, babies need a bottle at least once every four hours. She's had one at around seven, so she'll need to drink again at eleven, and then at three a.m. And so forth."

"That's a lot of work. I'm glad I used to leave all that business to my wife. Alas, I can't thank her for it anymore," Evert said with a wry smile. "On second thought, maybe it wasn't such a good idea, taking that baby carriage. It was just an impulse. I thought it was funny." Neither of us spoke. "Jesus, what an idiot I am sometimes."

"Yes, that's true," I said benignly. "Be that as it may, the point now is to contain the damage as much as possible. We did manage to get...uh...What's the kid's name, anyway?"

"Hey, completely forgot to ask," said Evert.

"Maybe you should go back and inquire."

"I think Christina would be an appropriate name, in the interim," Evert proposed.

We thought it over for a moment in silence. Then I went on, "But what I was going to say is that we did manage to get Christina to sleep. Good for us. And we managed to get nearly a whole bottle into her. Not bad. We even managed to change her diaper, although it must be said it's much easier now than it used to be, when you were dealing with cloth diapers and safety pins. It isn't even that much worse for the environment, apparently, in the long run. Because it takes more energy to get those cloth diapers clean again, than to—"

"Yeah, yeah, so what? The environment's not my problem, I won't be alive to see it."

"But maybe Christina will." I wasn't going to let my good friend get away with throwing me off my pet topic that easily.

"Whoever's alive then will have to take care of it then," said Evert, "and whoever wants to stay alive now needs to eat and drink. Us two, for example."

"First the news, pal. Let's see if Christina gets a mention on the evening news, and then, over a stiff drink and a bite to eat, we'll discuss how we can get our little princess back to her parents as quickly, tenderly, and secretly as possible." I stood up to turn on the TV. It was a couple of minutes before eight.

24

Same Time—The Baby's Parents' House

The police car halted in the middle of the street because all the parking spots were taken. The city had instructed the town planners to deliberately underestimate the car density per household, to allow the homes to be squeezed even closer together. After around 7 p.m. it always took at least ten minutes to find a place to park.

The officer got out and opened the back door on his side, walked around the car, and then opened the other back door as well.

"Sorry, childproof locks," he apologized. "To stop detainees from jumping out while we're driving."

"I understand," Johan Verbeek muttered, walking around to the other side to help his wife out. "Maartje, we're here."

Maartje was staring blankly into space. Then, slowly, she got out. The policeman's arm automatically shot out to keep his passenger from bumping her head, and in this case it was just as well. Maartje, hanging on to her husband's arm, shuffled to the front door as if she'd aged forty years in a couple of hours. A curtain at one of the neighbors' windows moved. The officer walked a little awkwardly after the baby's parents.

"Will you be all right now?" he asked.

"Yes, we'll be fine, I guess. Thank you," said Verbeek.

"Two of my colleagues will be here in a couple of minutes. The doctor is supposed to be stopping by later on tonight, I believe."

"Yes, he's coming at around ten."

"Someone from the tech department is also coming to work on your phone," the officer went on, "he should be here any minute. You're staying home, I presume?"

"Yes, we'll stay here. Unless Sabine is found, of course. Do the police have our number, by the way?"

"Surely they must?" said the officer. "I assume they took it down back at the precinct."

"Yes, I think so." Verbeek gave it some thought. "I'll just give it to you again, just in case."

An old Mercedes that was hemmed in by the police car honked its horn impatiently. The officer gestured at the driver to take it easy. The car window was rolled down and the driver spat demonstratively on the ground. The woman beside him peered in the rearview mirror, tugging at her eyelashes.

Now more curtains up and down the street were seen to be stirring.

The officer took out a notebook and took down the phone number. "*Fam. Verbeek*," he wrote, and in parentheses: "*(baby!)*."

There was more honking. The officer shook the father's

hand. He didn't know how to handle saying goodbye to the mother. She seemed completely closed off to the world.

"Best of luck, then."

Language is so hopelessly inadequate sometimes. The policeman returned to the squad car without looking back and drove off. The Mercedes behind him gunned it a bit too hard, squealing away in a cloud of diesel.

Johan Verbeek fumbled for his keys. Which were in his coat. Which had been left draped over the baby carriage.

"Maartje, my keys are in my coat pocket, and I don't have my coat."

Maartje gazed at him blankly. No words could penetrate her fear and despair.

"Do you have your keys on you?"

No reaction.

"The house keys, do you have the house keys?"

Now she did stick her hands in her pockets, but a second later she clearly had no idea what she was supposed to be looking for.

"So then aren't you cold?" she asked perfunctorily when some of what her husband said had worked its way in.

Johan gingerly lifted her hands out of her pockets and reached his own hands in for the keys.

25

8:00 p.m.—Princess Margriet School

Harry was on his sixth cup of coffee and tapping his fingers on the table in the school's kitchenette, a cheap IKEA kitchen at least twenty years old. Elementary schools in one of the richest countries in the world have to make the furnishings last for thirty years—the authorized depreciation allowance for grade-school furniture—whereas every self-respecting corporate CEO has his office refurbished for thousands of euros at least once every five years.

Harry wanted to go home. But the building was still teeming with detectives. Two of them had left with a plastic bag full of possible evidence, but five new officers had arrived to take their place. They were combing the building from top to bottom.

"What are you looking for, anyway?" Harry had asked two detectives who'd come in for a coffee.

"We won't know until we find it," was the reply.

And the most outrageous thing, thought Harry, was that they wouldn't let him out of the kitchen. Someone was telling *him*, in his own school, where he was allowed to go. They wouldn't even let him go to his own damn bathroom. Everything had been roped off with red-and-white-striped tape. It had finally gotten so desperate that he'd had to relieve himself in the kitchen sink. Turning around, he'd seen a policeman watching him through the window.

There were coffee cup rings on the table. There was no point cleaning up, Harry decided. He didn't feel like it, in any case. It would only get dirty again. His own cell phone went off, making him jump. It was rare for anyone to call him, except his wife, and even then only for trivial questions.

"Van Staveren speaking."

"Ditto. Van Staveren speaking. It's your brother, Wil. Say, what's going on over there? You were on the evening news, man."

"Oh, don't even ask. The shit's hit the fan here. A baby's been kidnapped, it happened during the Christmas pageant this afternoon, so of course the whole place is in an uproar. I've got eight detectives or more swarming around and it doesn't look like they're going home any time soon. So I can't either."

"But what exactly happened?"

"They'd left the baby in the bathroom vestibule for a few minutes, and then, it seems, some old dude just waltzed out with the kid. Baby carriage and all."

"And they don't know why?"

"No."

"And there's been no ransom demand or anything?"

"No, not as far as I know."

"What kind of people are they, the parents?"

"What do you mean, what kind of people?"

"Well, what kind of people are they? Rich? Important? Anything special?"

"No, I don't think so. They must be well-off, I think. They've got a fancy car, anyway."

"What's their name, and where do they live?"

"Verbeek. And I think they live in Van Tellegen Street. I happened to overhear the father give the policeman who drove them home their address. Why, did you want to visit them or something? What do you want to know for?"

"Oh, just because. I saw it on the box, and I thought I'd like to know more about that."

"Well then, now you know more. You never call me normally. I didn't even know you had my number."

"So I'm interested for once, and that doesn't sit well with you either! Have the pigs found anything yet?"

"Just a raincoat, I believe. They fished something out of one of the toilets where the buggy had been, and I think it was a coat."

"What else?"

"Nothing else; they're keeping it zipped."

"Well then, Har, best of luck. I'll call you again."

"Yeah, ciao."

Harry hung up. He considered having a seventh cup of coffee. Two officers came in asking when the building was last cleaned, who the cleaner was, and from what company. Harry answered grudgingly. The officers walked out again.

"Could someone please tell me how long this is going to go on?" Harry called after them, but there was no reply.

26

"Those journalists drive me nuts. And the ones from the so-called quality papers are the worst. All they do is parrot each other, they don't give a shit if something's true or not," muttered Chief Prosecutor Stork, who had just finished watching the evening news.

"They're just doing their job," the mayor bristled.

"No self-critique to speak of. Always chasing sensationalism," Stork went on, grumbling.

"No, it's *your* lot that's bursting with self-critique, I suppose." The city's press officer, Olga van der Vat, never let a chance go by to express her true opinion, to compensate for all the empty blather she was expected to spout whenever a microphone was pushed in her pretty face. She, like almost everyone else, couldn't stand Stork. He turned out to be right far too often. There aren't many who enjoy being proved wrong.

"Press officers, by definition, aren't about the truth, they're only about image, my dearest Olga," said Stork. "*Our* lot don't put image first. Or the truth either, actually."

"And what *do* you put first, then?" Olga snapped.

"Catching crooks and putting them away for as long as possible. Surely you ought to know that, my girl."

That "my girl" especially did not go down well.

Mayor Schaarsberg Donk decided she should come to her press officer's defense. "Why are you always putting people down, Mathieu? For the next few hours, let's present a unified front, please. This is difficult enough to get through unscathed as it is."

"Perhaps getting through this unscathed isn't the point here. The point is that we have to find a baby," Stork remarked.

"The one doesn't have to rule out the other, Mathieu."

"What should I tell them?" the police press officer asked the mayor.

"Which of us is going to brief the press, anyway?" asked Olga. "Isn't it city hall's job to inform the citizens?"

"Jesus, here we go again." Stork sighed. "Surely it makes no fucking difference who gets to be the one to have nothing to say? Whether you have anything to tell them or not, it's always '*In the interest of the investigation we have no comment at this time.*' Period. What difference does it make who says it? You might as well play a recording."

Nobody spoke.

The mayor made a mental note to start working seriously on getting Stork transferred once this whole business was over. Preferably as far away as possible.

27

8:30 p.m.—Hendrik's Apartment

Neither of us had spoken for at least five minutes. That was un-usual. Evert was sipping a drink. I stirred my coffee. We both sat staring into space. The TV was still on. Every few seconds you'd hear canned laughter at something *TV Guide* denotes as "comedy." If people could have seen us, they'd probably have thought we were some kind of surrealistic backdrop to the laughter: two silent old geezers, lost in thought, on a sofa.

I stood up. "I'm going to make another call. Those parents must be going out of their minds with worry."

"What are you going to tell them, then?" asked Evert.

"That they don't have to worry. That their little cupcake will be dropped off somewhere safe tomorrow. That it's all been some sort of misunderstanding. An accident. That we're absolutely not interested in a ransom or anything." I looked sternly at Evert. Who nodded slowly.

"Okay."

I put on my coat. "Back soon."

"Yeah, see you."

★ ★ ★

When his friend shut the door behind him, Evert sighed. He took a sip of his Jenever and stood up. Quietly he tiptoed to the bedroom where the baby carriage was parked and peeked inside. Under the improvised blanket, a folded towel, a little head with a smattering of dark curls poked out. Christina was asleep, the picture of contentment. Her own little blanket and sheet were hung over the radiator to dry. Evert had to swallow, and then he returned to the living room. He took up a position by the window to wait for his friend to come back. "Humdinger," he muttered to himself.

28

8:40 p.m.—Princess Margriet School

The phone rang.

"Princess Margriet School, van Staveren speaking."

"Harry, it's Hetty. What's going on?"

"Well, what can I tell you? They're still plugging away at it, and it looks as if they're not going home any time soon."

"Who's 'they'? And what are they plugging away at?" asked the headmistress.

" 'They' are around nine detectives, and what they're doing exactly I have no idea, because they've instructed me to wait in the kitchen until they're finished. They've got everything blocked off with police tape and I'm not allowed to go anywhere. Not even to the bathroom."

"Yes, sure," she said somewhat impatiently, "but can't you tell me about any developments?"

"What sort of developments?"

"Well, any news about the baby, or anything? Haven't they found anything unusual at school, any clues to the culprit's identity?"

"No, not that I know."

"Stay there until they leave, and if anything happens, call me pronto."

"Yeah, but that could take hours," Harry sputtered. "I want to go home. I have things to do too. I can't stay here forever."

"No, you're not staying there forever, you'll stay until they leave," Hetty said.

"Even if it turns into an all-nighter?"

"Yes, in principle. I'll try and find someone who could relieve you for a few hours, if they haven't left by midnight. But if I can't, you'll just have to sleep on the sofa."

"What sofa?" said Harry, peeved. "There's no sofa here."

"Well, okay, you'll figure it out, won't you? Get a mat from the gym or something."

"I'm not allowed in the gym."

"You're always so creative when it comes to helping yourself, so just find a solution, all right? Don't forget to call me if something important happens. Talk to you later." And without waiting for an answer she hung up.

Harry cursed and looked at the clock. He was stuck there. Who knew how long this was going to go on for, and there was nothing for him to do. The school did have a television set, but it was in the teachers' lounge, and that was cordoned off with red-and-white-striped tape. He was racking his brain trying to think of something when the phone rang again. *Maybe Hetty's found someone to relieve me*, he thought, but immediately realized she couldn't have arranged it that quickly, even if she'd wanted to.

"Princess Margriet School, van Staveren here."

"Good evening. I've got an important message."

"Who is this?"

"It doesn't matter. It's extremely important. Listen closely. We will be dropping off the missing baby somewhere tomorrow morning. Shortly afterward you will receive a call announcing where the baby carriage was left. It's all been a misunderstanding, you see. The baby is fine. We don't want a ransom or anything. Would you be so kind as to call the parents at once, and tell them not to worry?"

Click.

They'd hung up. Harry sat there with the phone to his ear for a few seconds longer, his mouth hanging open. Then he put down the receiver.

He feverishly tried to think what he should do now. Definitely call the parents, anyway. But should he alert the police as well? The caller had said nothing about that. If he told the cops about the call now, one thing was certain: He would still be here in the morning. He could always say the caller had ordered him not to get the police involved. Anyway, the parents should be called first. The number... Where had he put their number? He wasn't sure.

29

8:55 p.m.—Hendrik's Apartment

I was just stepping out of the elevator when the door of the apartment next to mine opened and a flushed female face belonging to a blonde in her fifties appeared around the door.

"I think to myself, I think, what on earth is going on next door? So I think to myself, I really must ask Mr. Groen about it."

"Good evening, Gerda. What do you mean, what's going on? There's nothing going on, why? Just having a friend over. He often comes over for a visit." I can be quite a good actor if I try.

"Well, I thought to myself, what's all the to-ing and fro-ing in the corridor about? And the elevator going up and down...I thought, I'll just see if I can be of any help to my neighbor." Gerda, on the other hand, was a lousy actress.

"Thanks, that's very kind of you, but that's all right, we can manage. Good night, and sleep well, won't you?" Calmly I opened my front door, looked back for a second, gave her a friendly nod, stepped inside, and closed the door behind me. Then I squinted through the peephole to see what she would do next. Gerda stood in her doorway with the phony smile on her face for a moment longer, then her face fell and she went back inside.

★ ★ ★

"Doesn't that broad drive you crazy?" Evert asked.

"There are people you just have to put up with. She does live here, after all. The best way to deal with her is to be very friendly and polite. That way she can't get her claws into you. I have other neighbors who are very nice people, you know. It's so seldom that I ever hear a peep out of that Turkish family on the other side, for instance, that I wonder if they're ever home."

"Oh, you and your diplomacy! You think you can solve any problem with fancy words and letters to the editor, but that won't get you anywhere. That neighbor just needs a good shellacking," Evert muttered.

"How do you mean?" I inquired archly. Evert was already opening his mouth to give a detailed description, but I put my hand up. "Keep the technical details to yourself. And let me continue writing my genteel letters to the editor. At least that's something. One person writes a letter, and the other works off his frustrations by coming home with a baby."

Evert had nothing to say to that, which didn't happen often.

"Anyway, I made the call and told them to tell the parents they shouldn't worry."

"Who'd you speak to?"

"Someone from the school, I think."

"And what did you say?"

"That it's all a misunderstanding and that the baby will be left somewhere safe tomorrow morning and that we'll call to tell them where she is."

"Did you mention a time?"

"No," I said hesitantly, "I didn't think of that. How are we going to handle it, in fact?"

"Well, we'll simply handle it."

"*Simply?* How?"

30

At ten o'clock sharp, the two press officers took their seats behind a battery of microphones.

Mathieu Stork watched the scene disdainfully from the sidelines. A ludicrous sight, as always, that row of mics with their little press logos. You could barely make out the speakers behind them. Couldn't it just be cut down to one camera and a single microphone? After all, there's no more than one answer to every question. No, they were all determined to lug their own equipment around to record this farce. As if the folks at home ever paid any attention to the labels on the microphones anyway.

It made Stork crabby. He had just called his wife to tell her he'd be late. His disgust with the inevitable Punch and Judy show had become so irksome of late that it was getting harder and harder to take himself and his profession seriously. He was aware that his cynicism left little room in him for anything else. He'd recently decided that he would work for another three years, then take himself off to a little cottage in Scotland and leave all the bullshit behind. He sometimes wondered if he wasn't too jaded to still be capable of being happy. He'd just turned fifty. Thirty more years to go, according to the life expectancy tables. He shuddered to think of it sometimes. His love for his wife was the only thing keeping him going.

The police press officer began to read a statement. A baby had gone missing, possibly a kidnapping, and the police were doing all they could to solve the case as quickly as possible.

Next came the opportunity for stupid questions. The assembled press made full use of it. What time did they discover the baby was missing? And who was it who'd discovered it? How old is the kid? Doesn't it need be fed? How are the child's parents doing? Do the police have a lead on the culprit or culprits yet? Might religious motives play a role in this? And so it went on for a while.

Twelve times the press officer stated, with nary a trace of embarrassment, that, pertaining to that particular question, in light of the investigation it was impossible at this time to comment.

A reporter asked if there was any truth to the rumor that the scuffle between police and a group of young men had had anything to do with the abduction.

"I can't comment on that at this time, except to say it may have something to do with obstructing an ongoing investigation."

Stork could already see the headline in *De Telegraaf*: GANG INVOLVED IN LITTLE JESUS KIDNAPPING.

Twenty minutes later the press conference was over.

★ ★ ★

At the postmortem discussion by the crisis team—consisting of the mayor, the chief of police, and the prosecutor—the mayor determined with barely concealed satisfaction that the damage to the city's image had been contained for now, thanks to her shrewd handling of the matter.

"Well, congratulations then," said Stork.

Chief Graven stared at him, eyebrows raised.

"Do you yourself have any children, by the way?" Stork asked the mayor innocently.

31

The "Botenbuurt" or "Boat-quarter" arose in the 1960s to accommodate young couples who, after years of living with their parents or in-laws in nineteenth-century working-class housing, would kill for the chance to move into their own thin-walled, dreary three-room flat in some hard-to-reach suburb. After seven to eight years of that, the ones who'd had enough of a pay raise to afford it would exchange their rental for a home in a brand-new housing development in watery new cities like Almere, Purmerend, or Breukelen, a homeowner's paradise of row houses with fenced yards meant for those who'd managed to score a piece of the growing prosperity pie. Today the only people who still live there are native Dutch who can't afford anything else, as well as immigrant Turkish and Moroccan families, and a smattering of seniors who were left behind. And Wil van Staveren and his wife. They hated everything and everyone, themselves excepted. Their main occupation was complaining. About the weather, about foreigners, about the referee, about the euro, about the rest of the world, and about each other.

Wil stared into space, chewing on a hand-rolled cigarette. He was thinking. He didn't do that very often. Not when spouting his opinion about something, anyway. His wife had fallen asleep in her chair, her mouth half open. Her considerable girth was stuffed into her Naugahyde armchair. Her upper dentures lay next to the pack of cigarettes on the glass coffee table, which also supported her feet. On the TV, *Big Brother* contestants were busy making one another's lives hell. Wil didn't see or hear a thing, so lost in thought was he, pondering his genius idea. There was just one piece missing: how to stash the bag with the cash somewhere without anyone noticing?

"Look," he told himself, "theoretically, of course, I'm not running a risk. I'm just doing my job: emptying trashcans. But I'll have to smuggle the bag out of my truck somehow before I get to the dump." He picked his nose and swallowed the proceeds.

"Enjoy," he heard. His wife had woken up and was gazing at him.

"Look who's talking."

"Me? Never."

"Did you get a beer?"

"Yeah."

"Can you get me one?"

"Do you have polio?"

"No, *I* worked today. Which isn't something you can say you've done for the past twenty years."

"Well, if you ask me, that 'work' of yours mainly consists

of drinking tons of beer. Actually, you're doing overtime now. Except that you're not getting paid for it here."

Wil let that pass. His wife hauled herself out of her chair and shuffled to the kitchen. Then she shuffled back to the living room with a can of beer and a bag of chips.

"Here you are, sir."

Wil was jolted from his reverie. He had just come up with the solution. Now he'd have to make a phone call. He had already looked up the number of the Verbeeks in Van Tellegen Street in the phone book, and had jotted it down on a piece of paper, which was in his pants pocket. He got up to put on his shoes.

"*Now* what are you going to do?" his wife asked, surprised.

"Taking the dog out for a walk," said Wil, with as much nonchalance as he could muster.

"She's just been out, and I just got you a beer. Are you feeling all right?"

"No, I'm not feeling all right, all right? Having to look at your dentures that you always leave out on the table is making me sick, and I just feel like taking the dog out for a walk."

"Can I help it if they make my mouth hurt? That dentist really screwed up. Those dentures don't fit."

"You might consider using a toothbrush once in a while." Wil straightened and grabbed the leash. A fat little white dog came waddling up. Wil had wanted a pit bull or a Doberman, but his wife had come home with this ugly, unpedigreed mongrel through an ad at the convenience store. He stepped out onto the building's walkway, pulling the dog on her leash behind him. "Come on, Lulu, get a move on!"

32

"No, I don't have any children," Mrs. Schaarsberg Donk, the mayor, said icily. "Why do you ask?"

"Just interested, Simone, I was just interested," said Stork patronizingly.

"Just keep your interest to yourself."

There was a knock at the door. Chief Graven, who'd been uncomfortably watching the exchange between the mayor and prosecutor, jumped at the chance to get up and open the door. The police officer who came in wished each of the three officials in turn a good evening.

"Same to you," said Graven, "now spit it out."

"A phone call, or, rather, two phone calls, have come in to the parents' phone. But they're quite different in their message. The first caller said it was all a misunderstanding, the entire abduction, and the second call was a ransom demand for a hundred thousand euros."

Mrs. Schaarsberg Donk's mouth fell open. Stork frowned. All Graven was able to bring out was a shrewd "Huh?"

"Was there a tap on the parents' phone?" asked Stork.

"Not yet. The men were just on their way to do it," said the officer, nervously rocking on his heels.

"Have the parents fetched and brought to my office as soon as possible," said Graven.

"It may be better to let them stay home, Wiebe," said Stork, "in case of another phone call. Not such a good idea, really, if one of your officers were to answer it."

"Hmm, you may be right. It's best if they stay home." To the policeman in the doorway he went on: "Send Zwarthoek to the parents' house, with Drijver, and let them know I'm coming over myself."

"Perhaps you could send a female officer, for the mother, Wiebe," Stork suggested.

Jesus, how come that man is so often right? the mayor thought to herself bitterly.

33

"So we agree it would be best if we could just tuck our little guest warmly into her carriage right this minute and drop her off somewhere convenient. But there are two drawbacks to that plan. One: both the baby carriage and the blanket are still wet through. Two: we have a neighbor spying on us next door, and there's a good chance she'll catch us." I puffed at the cigar I'd allowed myself for this special occasion. To guard against the baby inadvertently inhaling the secondhand smoke, I kept my hand outside the balcony door, which was slightly ajar, and blew the smoke outside. Bas, taking advantage, had squeezed his fat feline body back inside through the gap.

Evert, pinching his nose shut, was trying to push the cat back outside, but the animal wouldn't budge.

"Jesus, Henk, I'd rather have ten cigars in here than that smelly beast. If his stench gets into the curtains, you'll never have visitors again."

"I hardly ever have visitors."

"What about me?"

"You're not a visitor, you're a friend. And friends don't mind trading a little funky smell for the pleasure of my company."

"A little funky smell? Man, I'm horribly allergic to cats."

"You're such a drama queen." I stubbed out my cigar, put Bas back out on the balcony, and closed the door. "There, he's out. You can breathe again. Where were we?"

"*When* are we going to drop off the baby? *How* are we going to drop off the baby? And *where* are we going to drop off the baby?"

"How do you mean, how?"

"Well, don't you think a baby buggy's a little conspicuous? Maybe we should hide little Christina in a big box or something. Or in a shopping bag, I don't know."

"It seems to me it's best not to leave her anywhere until it's light out. Otherwise we risk them not finding her quickly enough," I remarked.

"Yes, but then people will also be able to see *us* more clearly as we drop her off somewhere. To give a description of us, and such."

"Yeah, that's certainly a drawback."

"I think that if we tell them precisely where she is, and as long as we wrap her up nice and warm, we don't have to worry about her not being found in time."

"Okay, agreed," I said. "Let me try to figure it out. It is now . . . ten fifteen. We'll give Christina a bottle around midnight, and change her diaper. By that time Gerda is probably still waiting behind her door, but I don't think she'll have the stamina to stay there all night. So around four or five a.m. we'll give our little guest her last bottle, and then we'll smuggle her out of here."

"And where are we going to leave her?" asked Evert.

"Um...let me think."

"Not near the same tunnel, anyway," said Evert. "Chances are there'll be a few cops lurking in the bushes there. Or some more of those young punks."

"Actually, I'd be surprised to see any youngsters on mopeds in that tunnel at six a.m."

"Mopeds? Who calls a thing that goes fifty miles an hour and makes the racket of a Formula One racecar a 'moped'? Well, never mind. Where are we going to drop off Christina?"

A momentary silence.

"There's another underpass a little farther on," I suggested.

Evert was thirsty, I was in the mood for another cigar, and we still didn't have a plan.

"Doggonit!" Evert cried suddenly. "Mohammed!"

"What about Mo?"

"He has to be let out. I totally forgot about my little Mo. I've got to run home."

"Can't a dog ever skip getting let out?" I asked.

"Well, not this one anyway. If I don't hurry up, I'll find a massive turd on the welcome mat."

"You can borrow my bike," I offered.

"Okay, Groen, take good care of our baby. I'll be back in an hour."

34

"We're done, for the time being, anyway."

About goddamn time, Harry thought to himself. "Well, that's good then," he said aloud. "We'll get home before midnight, anyway. Is there anything more you need me to do?"

"Make sure no one gets into the building until tomorrow morning," said the detective in charge.

"What time are you planning to be back here again, then?"

"We don't know yet, but you may assume it will be early."

"How early is early?"

"That I can't tell you, sir, but I don't think it'll be before seven. Would you please make sure you can be reached? We have your number and we'll call before we come. Have there been any other calls, by the way?"

"No, not really." Harry was very bad at lying.

"Still, I'm sure I heard the telephone at least twice."

"That was my wife. Wondering why I wasn't home yet. I'll pass her on to you next time."

"No, never mind," said the policeman. "Please give me a key to the front door and the code for the alarm."

The custodian complied with this request with barely concealed resentment.

"You may lock up now. I would advise you not to speak to the press, although that's up to you, naturally. I'll see you in the morning. Have a good evening."

"Good *night!*" Harry grumbled.

The last four detectives strode to the front door, unceremoniously barreling their way through a cluster of journalists who didn't step aside quickly enough, closed the door, and headed for their cars without giving them the time of day. After a brief huddle with the two remaining officers in uniform, who were stationed in their patrol car in front of the school, they were off.

Harry was alone.

"What should I do now?" he wondered out loud. He went over the events of the past few hours in his mind. First the phone call from Hetty. Then the call from the kidnapper, who had told him to contact the parents. The parents were close friends of Esther's, the gym teacher, and as luck had it, Esther had previously given him the parents' address and phone number so that he could discuss the upcoming Christmas pageant with them.

He'd used his own cell phone to call the Verbeeks a few minutes later, but with the caller ID blocked. He'd shut himself in a closet and disguised his voice, speaking through a toilet paper roll. That way he couldn't be fingered. And if they did happen to find out, he could tell them it was on the kidnapper's orders. The only way they'd find out the truth was if the kidnapper called again in the morning. Therefore, it was best for him to be the one to answer the school's phone; that way nothing could go wrong. Then he'd just tell the police where the kidnapper had left the baby, so that they could go pick it up and alert the parents. So no real harm done. In hindsight, it might have been better to tell the police right away. But then he'd probably have been made to stay at the school all night. Now he just had to get up very early tomorrow morning. He'd have to get back by six, six thirty at the latest. There was no way the kidnapper would call earlier than that.

Harry turned off the lights, punched in the alarm code, and slipped out the front door. He barely made it to his car, having to elbow his way through a throng of pushy reporters. One of them offered him two hundred euros for information, and to his great chagrin he kept his mouth shut. He knew it would have cost him his job, but he did curse bitterly to himself all the way home.

35

Same Time—The Baby's Parents' House

Maartje Verbeek lay stretched out on the couch under a tartan blanket. They'd given her some Valium, and this was the first time in hours that her thin frame had stopped shivering and shaking. Her eyes had rolled up and her eyelids were closed. She had insisted on lying down next to the phone, and nobody dared suggest carrying her into the bedroom. The doctor was standing in the middle of the room, wondering if he could in all decency leave now, or if he should stay a little longer. Johan Verbeek was perched on the edge of the couch. He kept shaking his head. A female officer was posted at the door, and two men from the tech division were working on the telephone.

Chief Graven wondered what he was doing there, other than showing by his physical presence that the case was the police's number one priority. The father's statement had been taken down, and was as good as useless. The man was so befuddled by the two conflicting phone calls that he'd been able to give very little helpful information. The first caller had struck him as being an older man; the same for the second. Big help, that. What they'd said exactly, he couldn't remember. It came down to the first caller telling him the abduction had been a mistake, and the second caller, shortly thereafter, demanding a hundred thousand euros. Both had ended with the promise of another call in the morning. There was hardly any point in staying here all night waiting for it. The father should be instructed what to say in case one of the men called back, but other than that, there wasn't anything for them to do.

An officer came in asking what he should do about the reporters at the door. Graven wished he could tell him to just grab a few cameras and microphones at random and smash them to bits, but, granted, that wasn't a real option. "Just ignore them for now, put up some tape, and tell them they have to stay at a safe distance." He wondered how the media could possibly have found out the parents' address so quickly. It didn't occur to him that all they'd had to do was follow his own police car. Graven was starting to hate journalists. Even now there were a couple of photographers on the roof of one of the houses across the street, hoping to get the first shots of the distraught parents. And then blather about freedom of the press if anyone tried to stop them.

"Do you need me to stay?" asked the doctor.

Graven turned to the father. "Do you think the doctor needs to stay?"

The father shook his head slowly.

When the doctor had left, Graven turned to the tech crew. "Is it done?"

"Yes, the phone is tapped."

"Why did it take so long for you to get here?"

"Because nobody told us to come."

Graven, realizing he was the one who had failed to tell them, said nothing more.

For a long time no one spoke.

The kidnapped baby's father shook his head.

The two tech unit officers left without a word, just a hand raised in farewell.

The refrigerator started humming.

Graven looked around.

The female officer standing watch at the door was trying to lean her back against the wall inconspicuously.

The father shook his head.

His wife groaned softly.

The telephone rang.

Graven jumped. Verbeek almost fell off the edge of the couch. The female officer walked over to the phone, then hesitated.

"Pick it up as calmly as you can," the chief told the father.

"Verbeek here." He articulated it as if his own name surprised him. He listened to the person on the other end of the line. Then he hung up without a word.

"That was a reporter."

"Flip-ping hell!" Graven drew the words out slowly, like a long sigh.

36

I was bent forward, my reading glasses on my nose, carefully inspecting the baby's little buttocks close up for any remaining poop.

"So, Sherlock Holmes, see anything?" Evert asked, grinning.

My friend was looking on, filled with admiration. Little Christina also seemed to have confidence in me, because she gave a contented gurgle, followed by a burp no construction worker would be ashamed of. "There now, isn't that better, little girl?" said Evert. We had given her a bottle until more was squirting out of her mouth than was going in.

A few minutes later she was tucked back in her sponged-off and nearly dry baby carriage, contentedly asleep. We had supplemented the bath towel serving as her blanket with a tablecloth, so she definitely wouldn't be cold.

"Quite a lot of work, though, isn't it, a baby," I said. I felt some sweat on my brow. I dabbed at my eyes.

"It's bringing back some old memories, isn't it, old pal?" said Evert, awkwardly putting a hand on my shoulder.

"Yes, a bit."

We stood there side by side, in silence.

I coughed. "I'm going to bed."

"Where am I supposed to sleep?" asked Evert.

"You can share my bed," I offered. "It's a double. One side hasn't been used in a while."

"How is your wife doing, anyway?"

"The same. A tender little plant. A broken little greenhouse flower. Drugged up the kazoo. I don't really know what would happen if she stopped taking those pills."

"Do you still visit her?"

"Once a month. I take her out for a walk, and then we'll have a cup of tea. There is still a small spark of recognition and a glimmer of affection. I'm getting used to it. It doesn't make me as sad as it used to. The doctor says she's making some progress, and he thinks we may try having her go home again sometime. In which case I'd have to move back to our house as well, since this flat is too small for two people. I kind of dread it, actually."

"What's 'sometime'?"

"The doctor couldn't really tell me. Six months or a year. Maybe longer."

Evert gave me something resembling a pat on the back. We were both quiet.

Then he said, out of the blue, "I've put my name down for independent living."

It didn't really register at first, and I must have looked

puzzled, because Evert clarified: "I've put my name down for senior housing."

"You, in senior housing? Among all the old folks? What's got into you all of a sudden?"

Evert looked pained, but explained: He had been to the doctor for his diabetes, and the doctor had told him that if he kept going the way he was going, there was a good chance he'd end up in a wheelchair.

"And what did he mean 'by the way you're going'? Drinking and smoking?" I asked.

"Indeed. Plus a rather unhealthy diet. So I told him I'd rather be confined to a wheelchair than stop indulging in the finer things in life. And that I'd always hated walking anyway."

The doctor had suggested that he sign himself up for a senior home as a precaution. I said that I predicted he'd get kicked out for misbehavior in no time.

"That's why I'm going independent, Hendrik. An independent flat. Not in the nursing home, but attached to it. And then it occurred to me, wouldn't my friend Hendrik like to come and live next door to me? I think you should sign up for one too."

Evert had sprung this on me so suddenly that for several minutes I'd forgotten all about our little houseguest.

"I'll have to sleep on it for a while. And that's what I intend to do right now, seeing that we have to get up bright and early. Are you coming?"

"I think I'll sleep on the couch, if you don't mind."

"Do I have cooties or something?"

"Well, yeah, sort of. Say, do you happen to have a clean pair of pajamas for me?"

I did.

We'd known each other for over ten years but we had never had a sleepover. Ours is a strange and very special friendship of two men with very different personalities. I am the very model of a law-abiding citizen, sometimes to my own chagrin, but that's just the way I am. Elementary school principal for many years. Well-read, sensible, cautious. I try to spend as little time as possible dwelling on the great tragedy of my life—or, rather, two great tragedies. My little girl drowned when she was four. I thought my wife was watching her, and my wife thought she was with me. She pedaled her tricycle into a flooded ditch.

My wife never got over it. She became manic-depressive, and she's been in a mental institution ever since her last deep depression a few years ago, when she threatened to kill herself. Her umpteenth stay. Since I couldn't bear living in our house by myself, a friend of mine arranged for me to move into this apartment. I have a three-year lease.

Now I spend most of my time fighting injustice by writing letters to the editor of *Het Parool*.

My friend Evert never reads the newspaper; he never watches the news on TV either. He is madly impulsive, by turns boorish or ornery. His wife died last year, and since his retirement, Evert, like me, has lost touch with the rest of the world a bit. He has two children, one of whom he has no contact with at all, and the other, his son Jan, lives somewhere in the south and doesn't come to see him very often, just at Christmas and for birthday celebrations. In order to have someone to talk to he got himself a dog, Mohammed, aka Mo.

If you asked me what we had in common, I would say: a strong sense of social justice. We met on the local Remembrance Day committee, advocating for a monument to the fallen. We complemented each other, presenting a formidable team that was feared by officials and local politicians alike. I threw my authority as school principal into the mix, penning impressively composed petitions; it's especially important for future generations to remember the war, after all. And Evert, by way of persuasion, would sometimes grab an official by the collar and yank him halfway across his desk.

After five years of effort, a monument to the war dead was unveiled in the local park. A rather mystifying sculpture, to be sure; only the words on the base give any hint that it has something to do with World War II victims, but still. It filled us with pride and created a lifelong bond between us. A bond that has for the past years manifested itself as a fortnightly visit from Evert to my place, and a return visit in the intervening week by me to Evert's. The program is always the same: cocktails, a light meal, and a game of chess.

Little baby Jesus had seriously disrupted our routine, with the result that I was now making up a bed for Evert on the couch.

"Do you have a toothbrush I could use, by any chance?" Evert asked.

"You can use mine, if you like."

"That's disgusting."

"I only have one."

"Don't you have anything else?"

I rummaged around in the kitchen cupboards and came up with a dishwashing brush. "Voilà."

"Oh well," said Evert, "I take my dentures out at night anyway, so it doesn't matter. Now the only other thing I need is a glass to leave them in."

We went into the bathroom. Evert took out his dentures, brushed them with the scrubbing brush, and dropped them in the glass resting on the rim of the sink.

"I usually use that brush for cleaning the toilet," I joked.

"Gross!" cried Evert. He spun around, and in doing so knocked the glass off the sink with his elbow. It shattered on the tiled bathroom floor, his dentures landing on top of the broken glass. A piece had chipped off. "Shit, *now* look what you've done!"

"I was just pulling your leg..." I must have looked so crestfallen that my friend couldn't help laughing. And without his dentures in, it was not a pretty sight.

37

Wil couldn't get to sleep. His wife seemed to sleep all the more soundly; gentle snores arose from her side of the bed. He got up quietly, took a beer from the fridge, and sat down at the kitchen table. He went over his brilliant plan again. For once in his life he'd seize his chance. Only...Maybe he should have asked for more. One hundred thousand euros was five years of his salary. Two hundred thousand euros was ten times his yearly salary. On the other hand, one hundred thousand was easier to get your hands on than two hundred thousand. They wouldn't have such a problem with a hundred thousand. A hundred thousand fits easily in a plastic shopping bag. At least...He had an idea. He began gathering up all the paper bills in his wallet. Emptied his wife's purse as well. Eight bills. He folded them double, making a stack of sixteen. He folded them again. Thirty-two. He shouldn't ask for it in hundred-euro bills. Fifty-euro bills, that was less conspicuous. He worked it out: Two thousand fifty-euro bills make a hundred thousand euros. Sixty rolls, just about, like the one he now held in his hand. Yeah, that would fit in a plastic shopping bag. It was also compact enough to fit in a trashcan. He took a sip of his beer and let out a contented burp.

38

"What time is it?" asked Mayor Schaarsberg Donk. "I wouldn't mind getting home."

"It's twelve o'clock on the dot," said the press officer.

"What's happening with the investigation, Wiebe?" asked the mayor. "Got anything yet?"

"No, I don't have anything yet. We've got twenty men working on it. Still no trace of the baby, just two phone calls from two different guys who both say they're releasing the kid. One of them wants nothing in return, the other wants a hundred thousand euros." The police chief fell silent, plucking at his police mustache.

"What gives, do you think?" asked the mayor.

"I think that the older guy, the one with the raincoat, wasn't thinking clearly when he took the child, and now he doesn't know what to do," said Graven, "but that's just a guess. There are other possibilities."

"Such as?" asked Chief Prosecutor Stork.

"Maybe he's handed the baby over to someone else, who wants to cash in on the deal."

"Cash in on the deal?" Stork repeated.

"Not a pro, in any case. A pro doesn't ask for a hundred thousand, a pro would ask for a million."

"Yes, it's almost an insult to the poor baby," said Stork.

"Could you please keep your sarcasm to yourself?" asked the mayor.

"I'm sorry?"

"Another possibility is that the one demanding the ransom doesn't even have the baby. Or the one saying he'll return the baby never had her in the first place. There are enough crackpots out there. But it doesn't really make a difference as far as what we can do about it."

"What, in sum, have we done so far?" The mayor looked at the policeman, eyebrows raised.

"We have interviewed at least thirty people who were at the school at the time. Result: Two adults and one child did see the man, but aren't able to give much of a description. We've knocked on some fifty doors in the school's immediate vicinity. Result: One person thinks she saw someone pushing a baby carriage in the direction of downtown, and another one thinks he saw someone pushing a baby carriage in the opposite direction. Tomorrow morning we'll continue. Another five hundred or so doors to go. Or a thousand. Further action: Make inquiries on the street where the parents live and interview their friends, family, and acquaintances. The school has been combed from top to bottom, but any clues left behind were already trampled by hundreds of feet. We found a raincoat presumably belonging to the suspect in a toilet bowl. Profile of suspect is being compiled. Not sure what we're going to do with it at tomorrow's press conference. And then we have arranged round-the-clock surveillance of the parents and the school. Finally, the press is driving us nuts. They've been hassling the parents, calling them constantly. I now have calls out to every editor-in-chief, and I'm hoping they'll be able to rein in their people a bit. That's all I can think of, for now."

There was a short silence.

"May I?" Mathieu Stork looked at each in turn.

The mayor nodded wearily.

"I think we're wasting our time. I think the baby will be returned on its own. The old man took the baby carriage on an impulse. Perhaps he didn't even realize there was a baby inside. He first tried to return the carriage surreptitiously, but something prevented him. Probably those juveniles, maybe something else. Doesn't really matter. Then it was a little late for another attempt that night. So he called the parents and told them not to worry. There's no other way to explain that call. So my advice: Wait a while, and do nothing."

"Impossible!" snapped the mayor. "Doing nothing is not an option. How do you think people would react? I'd be toast. No, this calls for a full, forceful response."

Stork gave a deep sigh.

"Oh go ahead, sigh all you like, Mathieu, but we really aren't going to sit on our hands."

"If it became known that we were sitting on our hands, we'd have a problem," the police chief chimed in in support of the mayor.

"The only problem, if you ask me, is that missing baby,

actually." Stork sighed again. He had all too often tried to object to so-called "forceful response" and chafed at the alpha males or alpha females calling the shots. At the short-sightedness. At the constant repeating of the same mistakes. At the slavish kowtowing to public opinion.

Mathieu Stork, chief prosecutor, had just about had it up to here.

"Press conference tomorrow morning at ten o'clock. I suggest we reconvene here at eight a.m. to review. If anything comes up before that, they'll tell us." She looked around the small circle. Nobody raised an objection. "Good night, let's try to get some sleep, if we can." She put on her swanky coat and was gone.

"What's the story with those boys in custody, by the way, Wiebe?"

"It's calm for now, but I wouldn't be surprised if we saw some protests tomorrow afternoon," said the chief. "I have four riot control squads on standby. We're keeping as low a profile as possible. And in the morning I'll announce the formation of an investigative committee to look into possible police misconduct."

"And apologies upfront?"

"The minister won't allow it, otherwise I'd already have done it, for the sake of keeping things calm. He called specially to impress on us that even in this case there can be no exception to the rule that we don't comment as long as the investigation is ongoing."

"Well, then you might as well give him a front-row seat to watch the protests," said Stork with weary resignation. "Good night—or, rather, see you soon."

39

Same Time—Harry's Apartment

Harry was standing at the window of his apartment, staring out. He wasn't sure he'd get away with failing to inform the police about the kidnapper's phone call. But he couldn't really see how he could have handled it differently. He should be in bed, but he was afraid his wife would wake up and start peppering him with questions. In the end he lay down on the couch and, after a great deal of tossing and turning, fell into a restless slumber.

Wednesday, December 22

40

4:30 a.m.—Hendrik's Apartment

It's just as well that a baby that's only a few months old doesn't have any concept of fear; if it did, little Christina wouldn't have been sucking so contentedly from a bottle being held by a rumpled old man with no teeth inside his puckered mouth, a three-day beard, and a disheveled head of gray hair. When I carefully asked Evert if he'd been able to get any sleep on the couch, he grumbled that when he'd finally dozed off, he'd fallen off, onto the floor. On top of his glasses. Which were now perched crookedly on his forehead.

As for myself, although comfortable enough in my bed, I hadn't slept a wink. I was now hovering over the kettle to whisk it off the burner before it started whistling. As soon as I judged the water was about hot enough, I made two cups of tea. Next I smeared two pieces of toast with peanut butter, handed Evert one, and bit into the other one myself.

"Do you want me to take her for a bit?"

"Shuur. Shnn I kin shee aboush my dechures."

125

"What did you say?"

"Za you kin go shu hell."

Carefully Evert deposited Christina in my arms.

Before turning in for the night Evert had tried gluing the broken bit back on his dentures: He'd wrapped two rubber bands around them to keep the two parts together and left them on a plate on the radiator to cure. Now he carefully picked them up, removed the rubber bands, inserted them in his mouth, and three seconds later pulled them out again— in two pieces. I hadn't even heard them snap.

"Oh no!"

"Elmer's Glue-All glues all. Only not for very long," I said, "and that means there's no arguing about which of us is going to have to make that phone call."

Evert stared at his dentures, thinking it over. "You hab any Kosh dabe? Tape," he repeated when I looked at him uncomprehendingly.

Christina let out an emphatic burp, followed by a little torrent of milk that dribbled onto my hand and shirt. I handed the baby back to Evert in order to dab the milk out of my shirt with some lukewarm water.

"We've got to go," I said some moments later. Evert was just jamming his dentures into more or less the right position in his mouth. He had taped the broken pieces together, but now they didn't fit right. It looked as if his teeth were dangling helter-skelter inside his mouth.

"Say something."

"She shellsh shea shellsh on she shea shore."

I had to laugh. The baby in my arms laughed too. Which instantly made Evert forget about his dentures.

"I'll get her dressed in her jacket and socks and mittens. And let's not forget her hat. Meantime, could you please look for a large carry bag in the hall closet?" Evert disappeared into the hall, returning a moment later with a large, fire-engine-red tote that said "*FCUK*."

"FCUK! That's so wrong! You can't put a baby in a FCUK bag!" I was genuinely shocked.

"It just stands for French Connection UK. It was the biggest one I could find."

"Hmm." I pulled the bag open and estimated the baby's length. She probably wouldn't quite fit. After giving it some thought, I fetched a pair of scissors from the kitchen and poked a slit in the lower corner of the bag. "That's where the legs will go."

We put a folded towel in the bottom, carefully lowered the baby into the bag, pulled her little feet through the hole in the side, and covered her with a second towel and a folded garbage bag. We stuck the little feet into two goat-wool socks of mine. To keep them dry, a plastic sandwich bag fastened with a rubber band. Two paint stirrers kept the sides of the bag taut. Christina gave not a peep and seemed very content in her new carry-crib.

"Try picking it up," I said.

Evert picked up the bag, walked up and down with it a couple of times, and then put it down again. "Perfect."

"What time is it?"

"Nearly five."

"Okay, we're going. You know the way?"

"I'm turning right, crossing at the red light, then following the bike path for about three hundred yards to the first underpass I get to. There I'll give Christina a little kiss and put her down under one of the ceiling lights."

"Right. Let's go."

We tiptoed out the door as quietly as we could and got into the elevator. On the way down I checked the shopping bag again. When we reached the ground floor I cleared my throat. "Now, good luck then, Evert."

"You too. See you later."

41

Harry woke up with a start. For an instant he had no idea where he was. Then it dawned on him that he'd fallen asleep on his own couch, and he remembered the events of last night. He had to get back to the school, in case the kidnapper called again. He regretted not saying anything to the police last night. It was suddenly making him terribly nervous. He sniffed his armpits. He'd have to go into the bedroom to get a clean shirt. He opened the door as stealthily as he could. The closet door creaked.

"What are you doing?" His wife's hoarse voice made him jump. She sat up, faint and shapeless in the dark.

"I'm getting a shirt to wear."

"What time is it?"

"Early."

"How early?"

"What does it matter? Go back to sleep."

His wife fumbled for the alarm clock. "It's five fifteen, Harry, and you're standing in front of the closet looking for a shirt."

He had an inspiration. "The alarm's gone off, at the school."

"Hey, since when do you care?"

"Since yesterday. Turn on the news in a little while."

"The news? How come?"

"No time now. Got to go."

Harry shut the bedroom door and in the living room pulled on the clean shirt and pants he'd grabbed. As he was putting on his socks his wife came in, in her bathrobe. "What's going on? Tell me!"

With unconcealed reluctance, Harry summarized the situation. "A baby's gone missing at the school, and the police are on their way."

"Here?"

"No, of course not. To the school."

"Hey, cool it, how was I supposed to know?"

"Forget it."

"No, I won't forget it! Is there something I can do?"

"No."

Harry put on his coat without another word, checked to see if he had all his keys, and went out.

42

Same Time—The Bus Station

It was gently raining. I had walked to a different phone booth this time, to be on the safe side, the one at the bus station. Now I was standing drenched and somewhat out of breath in the cell with the receiver in my hand. On my way there, I kept glancing over my shoulder, until I realized it made me look even more suspect.

An old guy making his way in a downpour to a phone booth at the bus station, at the crack of dawn before the buses even started running. Making a phone call. I couldn't help grinning to myself at the absurdity. Then I peeled the yellow scrap of paper with the school's phone number on it from my wallet. I rehearsed what I was going to say one last time, took a deep breath, and dialed the number. It rang five times, and then I heard: "This is the answering machine of Princess Margriet School. We cannot come to the phone at this time. We can be reached between eight and four Monday to Friday. If you are calling because your child is sick, or have another issue, leave your message after the beep." Oh Lord. Not for a moment had I counted on the possibility that there would be no one to pick up. If nobody picked up the phone, they wouldn't pick up the baby either: The baby that was now, in 37-degree weather, lying in a red shopping bag in some underpass. I heard a beep. I hesitated another moment or two, then hung up. I retraced my steps as fast as I could, turned left two blocks before my own building, hurried through a deserted neighborhood of single-family homes, and crossed the street into a small park. A few minutes later I arrived at the underpass. I could see the big red bag from a long way off. I increased my pace, finally reached the shopping bag, bent down, and gave a sigh of relief. Christina was peacefully asleep under her makeshift blanket, looking warm and snug. I picked up the bag, looked around, and carried it back to my building. I had to take care that the bag didn't swing into my knees, and so I had to hold it out, away from my body. After a minute or so the strain became too much, and I had to switch to my other arm. A few minutes later I was back in the elevator, panting like a dog, a burning ache in both arms. I had to lean against the wall in order to stay standing. With my last ounce of strength I pushed open my front door, dropped the bag under the coat rack, and sank down beside it, spent.

Evert's dentures almost fell out of his mouth in surprise.

43

Harry parked his car in front of the gate and hastily got out.

"Good morning, sir, may I ask why you're here?"

The officer who had suddenly materialized behind him made Harry jump. "I'm here to open the school."

"At five thirty?"

"Yes, your colleague told me to get to the school early."

"My colleague just told you to be sure we could reach you."

"Yes, that too."

"What are you going to do?" asked a second police officer who had joined them.

"Clean up the mess from yesterday, for one. Make coffee. Get everything ready. That sort of thing." Harry was getting nervous.

"Under no circumstance are you to go anywhere that's been cordoned off, are you aware of that?"

"Yes, I'm aware."

"Well, in that case go ahead. But first, move your vehicle

please. You're blocking the entrance." The cops returned to their own car.

With visible reluctance, Harry moved his car up thirty feet, then strode up to the school's front door. As he was unlocking the door, he was briefly blinded by the flash of a camera. Even at this hour, there was a photographer lurking in the bushes. He swore, went inside, turned off the alarm, and walked through to the kitchenette where the telephone was and the answering machine beside it. The flashing light indicated someone had called. He rewound the tape and listened. The answering machine announced a message had been left at 5:17 a.m. The message consisted of a short silence and the click of someone hanging up.

Harry realized he was in deep trouble.

44

"What time do you think a school like that's supposed to open?" Evert wondered out loud after ramming his dentures into place for the umpteenth time.

"Beats me. Seven thirty or so?" I suggested. When I was still working, I used to get to school early, to turn on the heat, make a little tour of the building, and get started on some administrative business. I used to love that quiet hour before the children arrived and all hell broke loose.

"Shouldn't someone have been there when you called? It's an exceptional situation, after all. It's not every day someone absconds with a baby."

"No indeed, Evert, it's not something you see every day." I sighed. "It was pretty dumb of us, though, to assume there would be someone at the school at five fifteen. But even dumber: When I got the answering machine, I should just have gone ahead and called the police. Dumb!"

"Only in hindsight, Henk. I think it was very smart of you, actually, to rush back and retrieve our baby. A new personal record in the fifteen-hundred-meter dash, I think." This lengthy utterance saw Evert's dentures again slipping alarmingly. He took them out of his mouth, removed the smaller broken piece, and stuffed the remainder back in.

"There, that feels better. I'll just leave it like that."

"What now? What do we do?" I asked, tapping my index finger slowly on the tabletop. "I think, actually," I answered myself, "that we should just try again, in a while. First let me recover a bit, then I'll go call again. First the school, and if they don't pick up, I'll call the police. And then let's just hope we don't run into anyone."

"I know how to get to that underpass now, anyway," said Evert, "and I didn't see anyone, so maybe it won't be different this time. What time does that ghastly neighbor of yours usually get up?"

"I'm not in the habit of keeping track, but I don't usually hear much stirring there before eight."

"If that one gets in the elevator with me holding a shopping bag with a baby in it, I don't know if I'll be able to talk my way out of it. Nothing comes to mind right now, anyway."

"Me neither...Maybe you should just say you're turning in something to the lost and found. That's closest to the truth, anyway." I looked at my watch. "Okay, departure at zero six hundred on the dot."

"Not very long, then, before we hit the road again with our little princess. In the meantime, does she need changing or anything?" asked Evert.

Little Christina was still snuggled in her FCUK shopping bag beneath the coat rack. I'd just pulled back the garbage bag a bit so that she wouldn't get too hot under her towel. "As long as there's no peep out of her, it's best if we do nothing, I think. Other than hope and pray it stays that way."

"You do the praying, I'll go put on my coat." Evert hoisted himself up from the couch.

45

Despite the cold, Harry was sweating considerably as he walked across the empty schoolyard to the police cruiser parked outside the gate. He'd rehearsed a few times what he was going to say, but once he was at the car, he'd forgotten it. The officer rolled down his window. "Has something happened?"

"Yes and no," said Harry. "I mean, I think it's best for you to know something. Even though I had to swear I wouldn't tell the police."

The officer looked at him, perplexed. "What are you talking about?"

"About the fact that the whole kidnapping isn't really a kidnapping, it was just a mistake."

The officer still didn't get what Harry was trying to say. "What's just a mistake?"

"The kidnapping. Someone called last night and told me it had been a mistake, and that he'd leave the baby somewhere this morning, so that it could be safely retrieved. And that I shouldn't tell the police."

Slowly it dawned on the officer that the man standing by his car window had just told him something important. He poked his colleague in the ribs. The other officer hadn't heard the exchange because he had his ear buds in and, leaning back, eyes closed, was humming along off-key. He sat up and quickly pulled the buds out of his ears. "What?"

"This gentleman here has heard from the kidnapper."

"When?"

"When?" he echoed, addressing Harry.

"Last night."

"Last night? And you're only telling us now? What time?"

"Around nine. I wanted to tell you immediately, of course, but I was explicitly . . ."

They weren't listening to him anymore. The officer at the open window had picked up the radio phone and yelled, "0-39 for HQ, urgent, over."

"HQ, go ahead, over."

"Who's in charge of the kidnapped baby case?"

"The chief himself, but he's not here."

"Beep him and tell him the school's custodian is now telling us he's spoken to the kidnapper over the phone. And that we're taking him to HQ so please dispatch another cruiser to the school pronto. Over."

"Ten-four, 0-39, over."

"And why wasn't the school's phone tapped? Over."

"No idea, I'll look into it, okay? Over."

"And out."

The officer got out of the car and opened the back door. "Get in, please."

"But the school's open. I can't leave."

"Then lock it up again. We'll see to the rest later."

With his tail between his legs, Harry shambled to the front door, locked it, returned to the police car, and climbed in. The officer pushed the custodian's head down as he was getting in, something Harry realized he'd seen many times on television. There was a camera flash.

Ten minutes later a police car from the tech department drew up in front of the school entrance. They had come to examine the school's answering machine, but they couldn't get in because they did not have a key.

46

Wil woke up in a sweat. He'd dreamt that hundreds of babies had been thrown in the trash, and he'd been ordered to sort the living babies and the dead into separate piles. Every time a cop came to check if he was doing his job, the piles would fall apart, setting off howls from the babies that were still alive. A pale, fat mother was searching desperately for her child among the dead babies. "They all look so much alike," she said, weeping. "Some have already been taken away," one of the cleaners said helpfully, to console her.

Wil looked down. His wife was gazing at him with sleepy eyes.

"What's the matter? You're all sweaty."

"Nothing. It's just too hot in here."

"I'm not hot at all."

"Maybe that's because you're so fat. You don't feel anything."

"Oh, go to hell." His wife turned her back on him.

He stood up and put on his old bathrobe and worn

slippers. He had to go down three flights of stairs to fetch the newspaper from the mailbox. That wasn't that bad. But then he had to plod back up those stairs again. He arrived at the top cursing and panting, left the paper on the kitchen table, switched on the electric kettle, and dropped an instant-coffee bag in a mug. While waiting for the water to boil he rolled his first cigarette of the day, lit it, and opened the paper. *De Telegraaf* had chronicled the kidnapping of the little baby Jesus in its own tastefully restrained style. Wil read the article but found no mention of a ransom demand. "*The police are in the dark as to either the culprit or the motive,*" it said. "Great, keep it that way," he muttered.

Wil did realize his plan would fall through if the baby was found within twenty-four hours; he'd decided that in that case he'd be out of luck, but he wasn't really running any great risk. He stood up to make himself a piece of toast and fill his mug. Then he took out pen and paper and sat down again. Writing wasn't his strong suit, but he didn't want to goof up when he called the infant's parents for the ransom demand. Fifteen minutes later his coffee had grown cold, his breakfast was untouched, and he'd managed to jot down the following:

Listen up, it's the baby's kidnapper again. I want one hundred thousand euros in unmarked fifty-euro bills to get dropped off tomorrow morning at a location to be advised later. Leave the money in a plastic Albert Heijn shopping bag. No hidden mics, no transmitters, or the baby is toast. And of course no police. You have to drop off the bag with the money yourself. I'll call later to say what time and where.

He read the paragraph through once more and was satisfied. He'd heard the business about the unmarked bills somewhere else. He was pleased with himself. He put his coffee in the microwave to heat and ate his toast. Twenty minutes later he was out the door.

47

Chief Graven came rushing into the station and, without further ado, asked, "Where's that maintenance man?"

"Interrogation room two," replied the detective who'd been waiting for his boss.

"Thanks. Good morning, by the way."

The policemen briefly agreed on a strategy, and then went in.

In interrogation room two, Harry was sitting on an uncomfortable plastic chair in front of a desk. He was flustered, and his coffee was getting cold. He realized he'd gotten himself into a bit of a mess.

"Graven, chief of police," Graven introduced himself.

"Van Staveren, head custodian of the Princess Margriet School."

Then the detective introduced himself as "Schenk," and the two officers of the law sat down across from the custodian.

"Mr. van Staveren," the chief began, "my colleague here tells me you were contacted by the baby's abductor last night.

Would you please tell me, as accurately as you can remember, what happened?"

Harry told his story. Graven asked questions and Harry answered them like a naughty little boy responding to his teacher. Humility, he'd decided, was the best course of action in this case.

What a nasty little suck-up, Graven thought to himself.

There was a knock on the door, and an officer entered. "Chief, the men can't get into the school because it's locked."

"Well, I did give them the keys, *and* the alarm code," Harry said, seizing the opportunity to show how cooperative he was.

"The men who were given the keys and the alarm code were sent home after escorting this gentleman to the precinct. Because there was another car already on its way to the school. Without the keys."

Graven had a hard time hiding his irritation at this level of stupidity. "Mr. van Staveren, would you be so kind as to give my colleague here the keys and alarm code again?"

"They're my own set of keys, I don't like to give those up," Harry objected, for form's sake.

Graven restrained himself. He had read this fellow like a book the moment he'd laid eyes on him, and now he decided he had not been wrong. "I'll have the keys returned to you immediately, as soon as my people have gotten into the school. They'll be there for the foreseeable duration anyway, so you won't be needing your keys any time soon."

"But I'd like to get back to my school too, so maybe I should go with them now."

"That won't be possible, I'm afraid. We have a few more questions for you, and then we'll have to take down your statement. It's going to take another two hours, easily," said Graven.

"Two hours?"

"Or a bit less. Or more. Hard to say."

"But then that whole time there won't be anyone from the school at the school."

"That's correct. But we're not allowing anyone from the school to be at the school for the time being anyway."

"That didn't seem to be a problem yesterday." Harry was feeling a little bolder, heartened by the fact that there had been no mention of his withholding of information.

"The situation has changed since then, thanks to the phone call you just told us about. In a sense, you're the one responsible for this situation—that's the way *I* see it, anyway," said Graven emphatically.

Harry had to swallow.

"The keys and the alarm code, please. And a phone number where we can reach the principal."

Harry swallowed again and cringed. He handed the officers his keys and explained in an uncharacteristically small voice the way it all worked.

There was an uncomfortable silence. Graven nodded at the detective, who asked bluntly, "Did you call the parents?"

Harry hesitated. "I had to. The kidnapper told me to. I wasn't allowed to tell the police, and I had to call the parents."

"And so you just obediently did as you were told?"

Harry had a brainwave.

"I did it so as not to put the baby in danger."

Graven and the detective exchanged a look.

★ ★ ★

A few minutes later found Harry sitting across from a plump female officer at a computer, who began typing his statement with two fingers. The custodian's entire story was already recorded on tape, of course, but it didn't do any harm to have a second version, Graven had decided, even if only to make the man sweat. He had instructed the officer to take her time, and to make sure to rephrase the questions on the tape in her own words. Harry didn't understand at first why his typist kept excusing herself every five minutes, but after the sixth clumsily phrased question that seemed strangely familiar to him, a little light bulb went off in his head.

Graven, meanwhile, was awaiting the arrival of Chief Prosecutor Stork and Mayor Schaarsberg Donk. The prospect of their company did not bring him joy.

48

"Hurry up, Evert, it's already past six o'clock."

"Just a minute, I don't know if the bag's going to hold." To test the strength of the tote bag, Evert was using one hand to tug at one of the handles with all his might, holding the bag down with the other. The handle tore off, and Evert toppled backward into the coat rack.

"Jesus, what are you *doing*?" I asked, alarmed.

"I was testing the handle of that piece of garbage."

"Why? It held perfectly well the first time, didn't it? Besides, we're not putting a horse in that bag; a baby weighs just a few pounds, no more than a couple of cartons of milk. You were pulling on it as if your life depended on it."

"Yeah, and now it's busted. Do you have any tie wraps?"

"What are tie wraps?"

"Never mind. Do you have any string?"

"We've got to hurry."

"Yes, I know, but I can't carry it like that, can I? Get me a piece of string."

"I don't have any string."

"Surely you do, everyone has string lying around."

"What for?"

"Well, for fixing a bag, for example."

There we stood, nervous and irresolute, in my flat's small front hall. The door was ajar. We should already have been out of there. Evert was gazing around, looking for something. Then his face lit up.

"Just give me your belt, for now."

"Then my pants will fall down," I sputtered.

"Then just use a piece of string to hold them up. Come on, give me your belt, I'll bring it back, don't worry."

I pulled the belt out of the loops of my rather uncharacteristically crumpled pants and handed it to Evert, who began improvising a makeshift handle for the bag by tying the belt to the two broken ends. After some fiddling, he tested the result a bit more cautiously than before and decided it would do. Gently, we nestled Christina inside the bag. She gazed at us wide-eyed but didn't give a peep.

"Okay, you can call the elevator."

I tiptoed out to the corridor and pushed the button, keeping an eye on the apartment next door to mine and wiping the sweat from my forehead with my handkerchief. Evert was carrying the bag with the baby in it and, by the look of him, was even more agitated than I was. A practically sleepless night and the stress of the last twelve hours were starting to take their toll. We got in the elevator and rode down, On the ground floor, I pressed the button for the automatic door leading to the front lobby with the mail slots and buzzers. As I stepped back to give Evert and his shopping bag plenty of room to pass through, the belt of my raincoat got caught in the closing door. I tried to release myself, but with no luck. Evert, who had stepped through into the lobby, saw me wrestling with my coat and turned back to help me. That's when the door decided to slide shut again. Evert, standing in the opening with the baby-bag, set his back against the door to prevent it from closing. The door immediately gave way, and Evert tumbled backward, hitting his head against the doorjamb as he tried to catch the baby-bag with his foot. In spite of that maneuver, the bag and its precious contents landed on the floor with a thud, and Evert's foot twisted sideways.

"Owww!...Goddammit, God...Jesus..."

The baby began to cry.

I tore myself free and heard my coat rip.

My pal tried to get up, but his legs buckled under him.

"Get back in the elevator!" I panted.

Evert crawled into the elevator on hands and knees, pushing the shopping bag ahead of him with one hand. The bag was now making a frantic wailing sound. The door slid shut, and with a jolt the elevator started back up to the seventh floor. Once there, I had a great deal of difficulty getting my front door open. Finally I managed it. I grabbed the bag out of Evert's hands, hastily carried it out of earshot into the living room, then rushed back to assist Evert, who crawled inside on his hands and knees and collapsed against the wall by the coat rack, ashen. I shut the door, but not before catching a glimpse of the neighbor's door opening a crack.

49

Wil looked around surreptitiously before entering the station, which should still have a working public telephone, as far as he knew. An observant traveler might have noticed someone looking around furtively, but no one was paying attention.

He slipped some coins in the slot. Next he took a piece of paper from his pocket, unfolded it, smoothed it out, and pulled a pair of over-the-counter reading glasses from his breast pocket. He read what it said one more time under his breath, then dialed the number. Someone picked up immediately after the first ring. "Verbeek here."

Wil put on a very deep voice.

"Listen up, Verbeek. It's the baby's kidnapper again. I want one hundred thousand euros in unmarked fifty-euro bills to be dropped off tomorrow morning at a location to be advised later. Leave the money in a plastic Albert Heijn shopping bag. No mics, no transmitters, or the baby is toast. And of course no police. You have to drop off the bag with

151

the money yourself. I'll call later to say what time and where. Okay, bye."

Wil slammed the receiver down. By force of habit he pressed the button for the leftover change, but there wasn't any. Then he looked around to see if anyone had heard him, saw that there was no one in the vicinity, and sauntered back out of the station, looking over his shoulder twice as he went to make sure he wasn't being followed. About ten minutes later he was back inside his own building, panting. He had to catch his breath before he could start the climb up. Two boys aged nine or so came hurtling down the stairs.

"Hey, hey, slow down. This isn't a playground. Running's for outside only."

The boys slowed down and stared at him.

"Yeah, what? What you lookin' at? Beat it! Get lost!"

"*You* get lost!" one of them yelled through the door closing behind them.

"Go back to whatever shithole country you're from!" Wil wasn't ever at a loss for a subtle response.

50

Maartje Verbeek was sitting on the couch, wiping her reddened eyes with a crumpled tissue and weeping almost soundlessly, with just the occasional little sob. Her mouth trembled. A little horizontal streak of dried snot on her cheek did not check the tears rolling down it. There was a glass of tea on the coffee table in front of her. Next to it, on a little plate, was a cookie. Both untouched.

Johan Verbeek sat next to her, every now and then putting a helpless arm around her shoulders. He was listening to one of the cops talking on the phone.

"Okay, yeah, I've already told them. But is there anything else for me to do here?...When?...I'll tell them... Yeah...I'll call as soon as they get here...Yeah, later." The officer hung up. "Mr. Verbeek, I've just been assured that the money will be here at nine tomorrow morning, in the Albert Heijn shopping bag. So you needn't worry. You'll have to sign a form for it later. Also, two detectives and a psychologist are coming over in a little while, to make some initial preparations for tomorrow. Are you okay with that?"

Verbeek nodded. "Perhaps the doctor should come and have another look at my wife." He glanced at the bundle of misery beside him, put his arm around her again, and told her softly that everything would be okay in the end. She nodded mechanically.

"I'll call the doctor," said the officer, then turned to tell his female colleague in a whisper to call the doctor. He gave her the number.

"Hasn't the school had another call from the other guy?" Maartje Verbeek suddenly asked.

"No, ma'am, not yet, unfortunately. But we're staying on top of it. As soon as someone calls, you'll be among the first to know. My fellow officers are glued to that phone, they're not leaving their posts."

"But they weren't, before," Maartje said slowly. Not as an accusation, more as a sad observation.

The officer could only nod.

The time crept by slowly. Every fifteen minutes an officer would ask the parents if they'd like a cup of tea or coffee. They did not. An hour later the guys from the tech department arrived. They chose a coat for Johan Verbeek to wear when he went to hand over the money. They carefully unpicked the hem of the lining, hid a minute microphone and listening device inside, and then sewed the lining neatly back into place.

"But the man did say: no mics and no transmitters," the father said, without much conviction.

"No, there won't be any in the bag with the cash," said

the technician who seemed to be in charge. "The suspect will almost certainly check inside the bag, so we won't mess with that, we wouldn't want to risk it, naturally. But he isn't going to frisk you, he'll be in a hurry, so we're hiding this microphone and transmitter in the lining of your coat. You don't have to do anything except keep your coat on, of course, but in this weather, that makes perfect sense."

"Can you tell it's there?"

"No, it's completely hidden."

51

Mayor Schaarsberg Donk breezed into her own office, the last to arrive.

She looks like she's spent an hour at the beauty parlor, thought Stork, who was still rumpled from sleep. He'd only slept a couple of hours; his wife had woken him at seven forty-five, asking if he wasn't going to work. He'd been out the door in five minutes flat, parked his car in front of Town Hall seven minutes later, and walked into the mayor's office at the same time as Graven. He looked around: designer desk, designer chairs, designer bookcases, designer wastebasket. A genuine Corneille on the wall. A pity it was hung next to an official portrait of the queen.

Graven had sat down at the conference table. In the mayor's chair. His face was tired and drawn. He too had hardly slept.

"You're in my chair, Wiebe. But never mind, stay there. You look like you haven't slept a wink."

"That's right, I didn't. Got home at two thirty, back at

the precinct at six, because the school's janitor confessed he'd had a phone call last night from—let's call him kidnapper A—and that he then called the parents himself to give them the message. Kidnapper A probably tried calling the school again early this morning—with no luck. That, incidentally, is the kidnapper who says it's all a misunderstanding. The other kidnapper, kidnapper B, called the baby's parents half an hour ago demanding a hundred thousand euros, to be delivered tomorrow morning in an Albert Heijn shopping bag at an as-yet-to-be-designated drop."

"We can't complain of being deprived of new developments, anyway, so early in the morning," said Stork.

"Nor of wisecracks from you so early in the morning," the mayor snapped. "What reason did the man give for withholding that information?"

"He said the man on the phone ordered him not to tell the police. But he strikes me as a bit of a shifty character. I don't really like that janitor, although I doubt very much he's got anything to do with the abduction. He thought he could get away with failing to report the call by getting to the school early, at six a.m., but by that time kidnapper A had apparently already phoned. There was one unanswered call on the answering machine."

"But what was he trying to achieve?" Stork wondered out loud.

"Nothing, maybe," said Graven, "but there are some that would immediately think in terms of a reward. I didn't get any sense of sympathy or empathy from him. Not until I put the words in his mouth; then he was suddenly drooling with concern, saying it was 'sim-ply *ter*-ri-ble for the parents.'"

"What do you think, Wiebe, which of the two kidnappers is the real one?" asked Schaarsberg Donk.

"I think..." The chief hesitated. "I still think it's the old guy who happened to be in the school, who took the baby in a fit of mental derangement and is now having trouble getting the child back to its father and mother without getting caught. To me that seems the most logical explanation, if logical is the right word here."

"Sensible words, Wiebe," said Mathieu Stork.

"Well, to be honest, you were the one who said it first, last night," the chief went on, "but I'm racking my brain to explain the other kidnapper. He must have something to do with it too, don't you think? So there must be some connection between the two of them after all."

"And so what are you going to do now?" asked Stork.

"Get an Albert Heijn shopping bag with a hundred thousand euros ready. There isn't much else I can do. That's what was decided, in consultation with the father. We've already found a bank that will arrange it, and someone to be a guarantor for the money. The bag will be delivered before nine a.m. tomorrow. The father will be wearing a raincoat with a listening device, to be on the safe side, but we're not taking any other risks, and we're staying well out of sight. I'm still in the process of arranging, if I can, for an 'old lady' or two to happen to be in the vicinity when the ransom exchange takes place. But it wouldn't surprise me at all if the baby was back in its mommy's arms way before that."

"So it's game over for kidnapper B if he then calls to give the location for the purported exchange," said Stork.

"We'd have to talk the dad into being crazy enough to play along regardless."

"Couldn't you just have a policeman act as a stand-in?" asked Schaarsberg Donk.

"Yes, I can hardly ask the father of the child who's still missing to be prepared to act as the stool pigeon for the fake kidnapper, in case his baby has been safely returned by then." Graven heaved a sigh. He went on to report on the status of the search, which had resumed. Stork nodded off for a bit, while Schaarsberg Donk tried to think how to put a positive spin on all this at the upcoming press conference. Out of everything that had been said so far, not one word was suitable for disseminating to the press, "in the interest of the ongoing investigation." How then could she convey that she had everything under control?

52

Wil was studying the day's work roster intently. He was scheduled to roll out of there at eight thirty in vehicle 23, with his usual partner, Rinus Schepper, one of the few people who could stand him, possibly because Rinus was even more self-absorbed than Wil. Today he was assigned to drive Route B.

"Shit," Wil swore under his breath.

"And a good morning to you too," said a co-worker who was studying the same noticeboard.

"I wasn't talking to you, asshole."

"Oh, excuse me, touchy today, aren't we!"

Wil did not respond. He was racking his brain to find a solution to the fact that he would be driving one route today and a different route tomorrow. Which meant he wouldn't be able to choose a trashcan for tomorrow's ransom drop on today's route. There was nothing else for it: He'd just have to waste his lunch break driving around in his own car to choose tomorrow's trashcan and figure out the timing. So then tomorrow, after emptying the can with the money, he'd head straight back to the garage, fish the ransom bag out of the hopper, hide it in his colleague Deelder's rarely used locker, and...Someone slapped him on the back, and he jumped.

"What are you staring at that board for, Staff?" said Rinus, who'd come up behind him. "Don't tell me you're trying to learn the schedule by heart. You don't usually give a shit."

"Fuck off, Schepper. I'm just checking to see what time we're getting to the McDonald's today. I forgot my sandwich."

"Forgot your sandwich? You never bring a sandwich from home, man," said Rinus. "You always buy fries for lunch."

"Yeah, that's what I like. What's it to you?"

"Just eat whatever you want, man. I don't give a flying fuck." He turned and made for the coffee machine. Wil cast a last look at the route schedule and then lumbered, lost in thought, to garbage truck 23, charged with collecting street litter and the contents of every public trashcan on its route. Tomorrow morning, when they returned from their route, he'd get Rinus to fetch their coffees so that he could fish the bag of banknotes out of the trash and replace it with another bag; then he'd quickly stuff the money into Deelder's locker. Deelder never used his locker because he'd lost the key—a key Wil had found and had been "saving" for him ever since. You never knew when something like that might come in handy.

Then, once he'd safely hidden the dough, he'd jump back in the truck to dump the rest of his load. It was convenient that the trucks drove in at the front end of the building and out the back.

Later, when the coast was clear, he'd be able to retrieve the bag unnoticed and hide it in his father-in-law's garage. His father-in-law never went in there anymore, not since he'd had a stroke and could no longer open the garage door himself. *So you see, a stroke can come in handy*, Wil told himself. *Gloves!* he suddenly thought; he needed gloves, so as not to leave fingerprints on the bag or the locker.

Wil decided his plan was nothing short of brilliant.

53

Evert was stretched out on the couch with his leg up. He had taken two aspirins but was still in agony.

"Maybe you should take two more, Evert." I looked at the swelling the size of a chicken egg that had formed on my pal's ankle. Evert followed my gaze, looking drawn and helpless. It didn't look good, and I told him so. "You'll have to go see a doctor, I'm afraid."

"Yeah, that's impossible right now, isn't it. Jesus Christ, if only I'd never made off with that damn baby."

"Ranting and raging won't get us very far, will it, and what's Christina supposed to think of your language?" This wasn't even very funny. "We've got to find a solution, one way or another."

"I don't see how. My leg may be broken. There's no way I can carry a baby to a park. I'm done for. You'll just have to call the police, and the parents."

"How long do you think you'll be going to prison for?"

"Don't ask me."

"Six months? Two years? Five?"

"I've got no idea."

"Neither do I, but it's worth thinking it over a bit longer before we have the police at our door, don't you think? Even if you're only given a short prison sentence, you'll never be able to show your face again anywhere without people whispering, 'That's the guy who kidnapped that baby.'"

We were both quiet for a while. Christina decided she'd had enough to drink and spat out the nipple. I got up, holding the baby up against me, her head on my shoulder, and patted the tiny back like an experienced father. Christina rewarded me with a burp and a little trickle of milk.

"As long as she's here, I'll just keep the same suit on. I might start to smell of sour milk, but I'm not keen on sending my entire wardrobe to the dry cleaner's."

Silence.

We didn't speak until I put the baby back in the carriage and said, "I'm going to call the school again, so that they can tell the parents not to worry. Back in fifteen minutes."

Evert nodded. "I'm not going anywhere."

★ ★ ★

The ghost of a smile came over Evert's face. He heard the door open and close. Then all was quiet. He hoisted himself to a sitting position and peered into the baby carriage. Christina was looking around, completely content. Evert smiled and started making the sounds everyone makes when peering into a baby carriage. "Ta, ta, izzn she a big girl, yeah, izzn she." His voice was an octave higher than usual, another thing that goes with talking to a baby. "It isn't your fault, poopsie. Everybody loves you. And Grandpa Hendrik's letting your mommy know she shouldn't get too worried. That everything will come out all right. Grandpa Evert may have to go in the slammer for a while, but hey."

Actually, he didn't much like that idea. It was bonkers, he thought, wasn't it, that it was easier to steal a baby without attracting notice than to give it back undetected? There must be a way to get it done, surely? Didn't they know anyone they could ask for help? The only person he could always blindly count on was Hendrik, but this time Hendrik was pretty thoroughly implicated himself.

The doorbell made him jump. For thirty seconds it was quiet. Then the bell rang again. Evert held his breath, as if otherwise he might be heard breathing. A long minute later he thought he heard the door of the neighbor's apartment fall shut. But he wasn't sure. He crawled ever so cautiously to the front door and listened, only to jump again, this time even more scared out of his wits, when there was a loud knock a few inches from his ear.

"Neighbor? Neighbor? Are you home? I heard you, you know. What's going on?"

He froze, praying the baby wouldn't start to cry. Soon afterward he clearly heard a door opening and closing. He exhaled. His heart was pounding. "Nosy bitch." His anger gave him a new jolt of energy. "I'm not going to let myself be sent to the clink by that old witch."

He scooted on his butt back to the baby carriage, then waited. Ten minutes later he heard the elevator door slide open and, a fraction of a second later, the neighbor's door open as well.

"Good morning, neighbor. I thought you were home, but I see that you were out. So early in the morning, eh? I thought I'd heard someone leave and guessed it might be your friend."

"No, it was me. Good morning too, by the way."

"But then why didn't he open the door?"

"Who?"

"Your friend. I rang three times."

"You rang three times?"

"Yes, I was hoping to borrow an egg."

"I don't have any. Just cooked the last two this morning."

"So he's still in there, your friend."

"Yes, I believe so."

"But then why didn't he open the door?"

"Maybe, uh...maybe he was in the shower."

"Well, I certainly didn't hear any water running. And I always hear it running when you're taking a shower."

"Well, I think...He's deaf as a doorknob, you know. He probably doesn't have his hearing aids in. Without them he doesn't hear a thing. Now if you'll excuse me, I'll...I'll just go make him a cup of coffee. Have a nice day. And sorry about the egg."

"But, Mr. Groen, what was all that noise this morning, out here in the hall?"

"I wouldn't know. No idea. Would you please excuse me now?"

Evert saw Hendrik wriggle around the half-open door into his own apartment. The neighbor took a quick step forward, but Hendrik was too fast for her and pulled the door shut.

Evert was not an experienced lip-reader, but even so, he could tell that his polite and usually oh-so-correct friend was roundly blaspheming under his breath. Evert put his finger to his grinning lips. Hendrik took off his coat, hung it up on the coat rack, went into the living room, and pushed the door shut with just a little too much force.

54

9:50 a.m.—The Neighbor's Apartment

"I still think something isn't right. There's something going on. He's acting weird. There's something going on in there. It just doesn't add up."

Gerda van Duivenbode had been talking to herself for years, mostly because nobody else would talk to her. The only people she still spoke with were the baker, the checkout girl at the mini-market, and her neighbor Hendrik Groen. Although the baker and the salesgirl never got much further than "Anything else for you today?" or "Do you want the saving stamps?" or, in a pinch, a sullen "Have a nice day."

"Doesn't have any eggs, doesn't have any eggs…Well, funny that he just *happens* to have finished the last egg this morning. Something isn't right."

Actually, Mr. Groen was the only one she ever had a normal conversation with, even if he did always turn down her offer of a cup of tea.

She measured a spoonful of coffee into the filter, ate four

cookies while waiting for the water to boil, and racked her brain for a way to get inside her neighbor's apartment.

"I simply *have* to know. He just isn't acting normal." She took another cookie and poured the water into the filter. "It couldn't be something criminal, could it?" She dropped three sugars into her cup. "I can't imagine Mr. Groen breaking the law. But that other guy, he's a funny one. I don't trust him." She poured on more water. Now she had enough for two weak cups.

"I already called the police twice last night. Should I call again?"

She put out food for the cat and called his name. But the fat black-and-white feline on the window ledge remained disdainfully aloof.

55

Johan Verbeek stared at the big raindrops slowly rolling down the window. He was looking but not actually seeing anything. He turned to his wife. She was seated on the sofa, motionless.

"Did you hear what I just said, Maartje?" She nodded. "That nice man called the school again. It can't be just a prank. No one would do that. We'll have Sabine home again this afternoon, or tomorrow. I'm sure of it."

"Yes, but what about the other one, the one asking for a ransom?"

"The police think he's bluffing. That the other fellow isn't the one that has Sabine. The nice one wouldn't have called three times already otherwise. He said they'd run into all sorts of snags trying to return her. He also said that he was very sorry, and Sabine was a good eater and hadn't cried at all yet."

"That's true, Mrs. Verbeek," the female officer chimed in.

"What's true?"

"That we think there's a very good chance the last caller will bring Sabine back."

"Oh, I thought you meant about the crying. Who else would know that she doesn't cry much? So then it must be him."

"Do I still have to drop off the ransom tomorrow if we don't have our little girl back by then?"

"Yes, no matter what," said the officer who seemed to be in charge.

"And what if we do have Sabine back?"

"Then there'll be further discussion."

"By who?"

"By the task force leaders. And you of course."

"Oh."

56

Principal Hetty Schutter had with chilly reluctance given up her office to the "crisis response team" put together that morning by the board of the umbrella organization overseeing the school, consisting of Board Chairman Eelco de Visser, the school's social worker, a forensic psychologist, and a woman who was an expert in childhood trauma. That's how she had introduced herself, anyway: "Mrs. Schouwenaar, child trauma expert."

These four were sitting around the principal's desk; the principal herself had to stand, since there were only four chairs. De Visser, who didn't suffer from an overabundance of modesty, had appropriated the principal's chair and was doing his best to project that he was in control. Only, it wasn't all that clear to him what kind of action was needed to assert that control. He had begun the morning by posting himself at the front door with the intention of sending all the children home, until a teacher had pointed out that some students would come home to a locked front door. At

172

which point the chairman had determined his presence was urgently required inside. The rest of the children were asked if there was anyone home to receive them, and if not, they were sent to a daycare close by.

Therefore there wasn't much crisis responding for the hastily mobilized crisis response team to do. The trauma expert started working out a plan for the children to make drawings of what had happened. The social worker and Hetty were kept busy answering the two phones, which never stopped ringing, with the comment that they had no comment, and that the school was closed. Both phones were being monitored, and if a kidnapper, whichever one, phoned again, the police psychologist was ready to take the call. No one had asked what he would say if he did.

Several teachers hesitantly asked if they could go home. They were given permission to do so, although not very graciously.

De Visser asked for a cup of coffee. Hetty tapped on the window, motioning Harry to come in. She'd called him at home and told him to return to school at once as soon as the detective informed her that Harry had been "released" by the police after giving his statement. Harry had had two hours of sleep and was looking terrible. He was ashen-faced and sick from stress and exhaustion, but Hetty would under no circumstance let him go home. At least she now had *someone* to boss around.

"Would you bring us some coffee, Harry? And another chair. Or does anyone want tea instead?" The social worker asked for a cup of green tea. Which was too bad for her, because Harry, who wasn't a fan of those gimmicky teas, didn't have any.

Hendrik Groen

De Visser, the chairman, seized the opportunity to show his decisiveness by demanding in a peremptory tone that the custodian tell his story again.

Harry swallowed. "Wouldn't you like me to fetch the coffee first?"

"It can wait."

"Didn't they say that in the interest of the ongoing investigation, you shouldn't talk about it?" the forensic psychologist unexpectedly came to his aid.

Harry, relieved, snatched the life preserver tossed at him. "Yes, of course, that's what I was about to say."

De Visser's face stiffened. He was deliberating if he should stand up to the officer but apparently decided there was no point, for he kept his mouth shut.

Silently Harry brought in the coffee and tea. Besides the constant ringing of the phone, nothing was happening.

Outside the building, the gathering members of the press stood shivering in the cold. The ten a.m. press conference had been postponed. With the school as backdrop, the various TV channels' top reporters went live to announce the breaking news that there was nothing to report. They took shots of the playground, interviewed some wandering parent who seemed to have lost his way, then threw it back to the studio in Hilversum.

Harry was sent out for sandwiches. The cameras whirred as he crossed the schoolyard. Head down, he refused to answer any questions. To be so close to basking in the spotlight, and not allowed to say anything! He uttered some profanities under his breath. Twenty minutes later he was back with the sandwiches. A journalist wanted to know what kind they were.

174

57

It was a touching domestic scene. Evert was on the couch, his leg up on the ottoman. He had the baby on his lap. I was in the kitchen preparing her bottle, peering over the top of my glasses to see if I'd measured correctly. I had. Gave the bottle a good shake. Dabbed a drop of milk on the inside of my wrist to check the temperature, and then took the bottle over to where Evert was sitting. I myself sat down to watch in my old leather armchair.

I heard the key in the front door lock but didn't immediately put two and two together.

"Mr. Groen, it's me."

The living room door swung open and Jennifer, my cleaning woman, a jolly, broad-hipped Surinamese woman in her fifties, appeared in the doorway. I'd completely forgotten that it was her day to clean. Her eyebrows shot up in surprise. Then down in a frown. Her jaw dropped.

"What have we here?"

Evert looked a bit sheepishly from the woman to the baby, and back.

"What's going on?"

"Yeah, well . . . it's a long story, actually."

"Well, in that case I'll sit down." She took a seat next to Evert on the sofa, turned to the baby, and began cheerfully cooing to it in Surinamese. Little Christina, who diligently went on sucking at her bottle, squinted askance at the newcomer. She turned from the baby to Evert. "I am Jennifer, the house cleaner—just call me Jenny."

"I'm Evert," Evert muttered.

"And you've suddenly become a father! Congratulations," she said with a gleaming smile.

"Well, actually, no, that isn't it," I said. "He's my friend, and he is the grandfather of this . . ."

"Oh, Hendrik, just tell her the truth," said Evert. "It really makes not a blind bit of difference now, anyway."

58

The case files were marked "*Kidnapped Baby Jesus.*" The amount of paperwork devoted to it was already, after less than a day, impressive. Two secretaries had been added to the task force, because the average cop's typing and computer skills aren't anything to write home about: The filing of a stolen bicycle report can take an officer at least half an hour. "Did you give someone permission to take the aforementioned bicycle?" That's the sort of astute question the police are supposed to ask. Hundreds of precious hours are wasted on the impeccable recording of petty crimes. Actually *doing* something about them would be too costly. The precinct police had recently confiscated a sign at the market on which the vendors had written "*In case of theft we'll call the ambulance first, and only then the police!*"

The police station was a hive of hectic activity. Officers and detectives swept in and out with folders. The phones rang incessantly.

Three men were sitting in the chief's office: Chief of Police Graven himself, Chief Detective Vink, and Chief Prosecutor Stork. "The heavy boys," was how the coffee lady referred to the trio.

Graven shut the door and addressed the others.

"Vink, what do we have so far?"

Vink cleared his throat. "Not a hell of a lot. A coat, presumably belonging to the suspect, a busted bike, presumably also owned by the suspect. A description, but a vague one: male, early seventies, five foot eight, normal build, balding. Area search has turned up nothing. Motive: no clue. Possibly simply disorientation. He's phoned three times to say the baby will be returned as soon as possible. That caller is middle class, well spoken, no accent. The two ransom calls, on the other hand, are from a man probably in his fifties, broad Amsterdam accent, not very educated. The calls came from different phone booths. We're tracing their location." Vink paused briefly and looked at the others. "And we've had almost thirty tips phoned in about suspicious old men. From a senior citizen shopping for baby shoes and someone offering a stroller for sale on-line, to a lady who was turned down when she tried to borrow an egg from an elderly neighbor. We're following up on every lead of even the slightest merit, but I'd be surprised if it led to anything. And that's all we have to go on so far."

"It isn't much, definitely," Graven agreed. "What about surveillance cameras?"

"We have a hazy two-second shot," said Vink, "from a shoe store camera."

"What on earth was he doing there?" asked Graven.

"He wasn't buying shoes. He just happened to walk past the store window."

"Oh. And what does it show?"

"Not much. An old guy in a raincoat pushing a baby carriage. It's hard to make out."

"What direction was he headed in?" Stork said, joining the conversation.

"He was on Rembrandt Street, walking in the direction of Jan Steen Street."

"I'm sorry, but could you point it out on the map?" asked Stork.

Graven fiddled with a computer, and sure enough, to his own amazement, a map appeared on the screen. "It's the first time it's worked for me," he said, sighing thankfully. "The high point of my week so far."

Vink pretended to be deaf and Stork looked the other way.

No one said anything. Graven gave a forced little cough. "Sorry."

Vink pointed out the school to Stork on the map, and then the shoe store, about seven hundred yards away. "The timing works out. He walked past the store at 4:34 p.m. Security camera timestamp. Heading east."

"How long does it take to cover the distance from the school to that store?" asked Stork.

"At a leisurely stroll, about six minutes. If we assume our kidnapper didn't make any detours, *and* didn't wander around in the rain for hours, *and* didn't get in a car, *and* doesn't live too far from the tunnel where the baby was to be dropped off, then there's a reasonably good chance that that man and baby are somewhere in that neighborhood," said Graven thoughtfully.

"I agree."

"Have any tips been called in from that part of town?" asked Stork.

"I haven't seen the list yet, they're still working on it," said Vink.

"Are there any other leads? Regarding the baby's parents, for instance?" Graven tried.

"Remarkably ordinary people. Exceptionally dull. Much too honest to have any enemies. No money, not much, anyway. I'll eat my hat if it wasn't a complete fluke that that kidnapper just happened to take their child."

"You don't have a hat, Vink," Stork noted.

"I do have a hat, at home."

"If you're quite finished discussing headgear, what's your thinking about the case now?" asked Graven.

"It's a funny business," Vink replied, frowning. "I think it could go either way."

"Thanks, that's very useful."

"I still think," said Stork, "that we should refrain from doing something. No one calls three times to say he's going to return a baby if he doesn't in fact have the baby in question. If we put fifty men on the case now, it will (A) be a waste of money and energy, and (B) make the old man panic and make him do things he'll regret. So what we should do is calmly wait for the baby to show up, and then apprehend the fake kidnapper as he's picking up the ransom."

"Our dear mayor isn't happy with that plan of attack—you know that, don't you, Mathieu? I can just imagine her telling the press, 'Ladies and gentlemen, as of right now we're doing nothing at all, we're taking a wait-and-see attitude.'" Graven sighed, feeling another pounding headache coming on. His breakfast had consisted of coffee and acetaminophen, and the effect of the pills was already starting to fade.

He went on. "Thanks anyway, gentlemen, and please keep me informed. I'm going to see the mayor now, and I think it's best if you don't come, Mathieu, for now, anyway. Let's just call it a difference of opinion, and it won't do anything to improve the mood. I'll see you before the press conference starts."

Graven sighed again as he left his office on his way to Mayor Schaarsberg Donk.

Mathieu watched him go.

"Who has the list with those called-in tips, Vink?" he asked.

"Braspenning is still working on it. Why don't you go see him? He's on the third floor."

59

Jenny the cleaning lady wasn't a very introspective woman. In her whole life she had rarely reflected about anything for longer than a couple of minutes. It wasn't deliberate; it was more or less innate. Although she did believe that mulling something over for too long wouldn't make it any better, for her, anyway.

She had listened with astonishment to Evert's story, only once or twice interrupting him with a great guffaw. Finally she said, "So there we are, gentlemen. Well, I do admire you, I'm simply blown away." In her Surinamese accent, the words had a musical ring to them. "Except that it's complete madness to kidnap a baby, of course, you haven't done too badly, the way you've handled it since. I have to hand it to you. Just too bad about the leg, eh?" I nodded and Evert muttered something. My pal appeared to be just as relieved as I was to see how calmly Jenny was taking it.

She stood up. "Let me just go call and tell them that everything's fine, and the parents really don't have to worry. Give me the number please, Mr. Groen."

"That's very kind of you, but I called only two hours ago to say Christina's doing fine, that we're just having some trouble bringing her back," I objected.

"But I'm a woman. That's more reassuring."

I couldn't argue with that. I gave her the school's phone number.

"It's better if you don't use your cell phone, you should call from a phone booth, otherwise they may be able to track where you're calling from," I advised her.

"You are both so smart! I feel I've landed in a detective novel," Jenny declared enthusiastically. "Don't you worry, I don't have a cell phone anyway."

She put on her coat and was out the door. "See you soon."

Dumbfounded by so much self-assurance, we sat there staring at the door until Evert remarked, "Now they'll be even more confused when they get a Surinamese matron on the phone telling them it's going to be all right."

"Oh, what an idiot I am! I forgot to tell her she wouldn't get the parents on the phone but the school. I've got to warn her." I got to my feet and pulled on my coat.

"Hey, Hendrik, as long as you're going out anyway, could you just swing by my house to feed Mo and take him for a little walk? The dog food is under the sink."

I said I would and dashed out the door.

★ ★ ★

Evert stayed behind, awestruck.

"Well, well, all that energy seems to be contagious. And it's all for you," he muttered, peering tenderly into the carriage. There was a knock on the door.

"Mr. Groen, do you mind if I disturb you one more time?" It was the neighbor.

Evert froze. "That bitch again," he whispered.

"Mr. Groen? Are you in there?"

60

Same Time—Police Station

Mathieu Stork took the stairs up to the third floor and asked to see Detective Braspenning. A female officer escorted him to an office at the end of a long corridor. Stork knocked, then went in without waiting for an answer.

Braspenning did not look up and went on typing slowly with two fingers. Next to his computer were some handwritten A4s.

"Yes?"

Upon closer inspection, Stork realized he knew this Braspenning. His last name hadn't rung a bell, but when he saw the pale face and greasy head of hair hovering over the keyboard without looking up, he realized it was Detective Bram he was dealing with. Slightly on the spectrum, Bram had originally been hired for his sleuthing talents, but somewhere on the career path he had lost his bearings and had never found his way back. In the end they'd shunted him off to a remote desk where his supervisor largely employed him as a far too expensive and rather mediocre typist.

"Hello, Bram, long time no see. How's it going?"

"Can't complain, Mr. Stork, can't complain." He glanced up briefly.

"Vink said you were working on the list of called-in tips, is that right?"

"I'll have it done in twenty-five minutes, Mr. Stork."

"Hmm, I'll have left by then. Know what, Bram? Why don't you go have your lunch and in the meantime I'll have a quick look at it."

"I'm not hungry." Bram scratched his greasy hair nervously.

"Then go take a walk. Get some fresh air."

Bram took a deep breath, debated whether to object, then gave up and put on his coat.

"What time may I come back, Mr. Stork?"

"In thirty-five minutes, Bram. And I'll tell your supervisor that I'm the one who suggested it, before he starts yelling at you."

"See you in thirty-five minutes then, Mr. Stork."

"Yes, see you later, Bram."

Bram disappeared without a sound.

The chief prosecutor dusted off the chair with his hand and sat down at the computer. It showed a list of seventeen calls. Next to the PC were some handwritten notes on more tips that had been called in. Stork counted ten of these.

61

Fifteen Minutes Earlier—Princess Margriet School

The crisis response team was experiencing a bit of a lull.

Sitting around the conference table in the teachers' lounge were Board Chair Eelco de Visser, the social worker, the trauma expert, and the school's principal, Hetty Schutter. They had nothing to manage except the phone. That instrument rang frequently, but it was invariably another member of the press.

"As regards the kidnapped baby, we have no comment at this time," was the standard reply the police had dictated to the principal.

Harry was sitting on a little stool in a corner waiting for the next tea or coffee request, or some other errand the others in the room were too important to handle themselves.

He was exhausted after his near-sleepless night. In an unguarded moment he almost toppled off his stool when his eyes briefly drooped shut. Hetty sent him a withering look.

Happily the attention was drawn from him because the telephone rang.

"Princess Margriet School, Mrs. Schutter speaking, good morning."

For a few instants she looked blank, but immediately thereafter started gesturing wildly with her free arm, panicked, pointing at the phone.

"Yes...yes, but...when's that supposed to happen?... Who is this, by the w..." She stared at the receiver as if it could tell her something, ending with a drawn-out, startled, "Well...!"

"What is it? What is it?" De Visser snatched the receiver from her hand and started yelling "Hello? Hello? Hello?" into it, to no avail.

"Who was that?" the social worker asked sheepishly.

"A woman. Surinamese. She said not to worry about the baby. That by tonight or tomorrow morning she'd be safe and sound in her parents' arms again."

"Well, that's good news. Isn't it?" De Visser gazed triumphantly around the small circle, almost as if this happy turn of events should be chalked up to his own leadership.

★ ★ ★

In the office next door, a detective took off his headset and dialed HQ.

"Hello, it's Uzcuk, let me speak to Chief Graven, please. ASAP. It's urgent."

62

"Mr. Groen? Are you in there?" Gerda van Duivenbode asked again.

She was sure there was someone in her neighbor's apartment. She could put two and two together, couldn't she? Hadn't she seen her neighbor herself, and hadn't he told her his friend was still there? She'd also clearly heard the cleaning lady arriving, at her regular day and time. But strangely enough, one of them had left again shortly afterward, and she'd have sworn it was the Surinamese woman; she could tell from the sound of the footsteps. Almost immediately after that, she'd heard either Groen or his friend take the elevator down as well. Gerda had feverishly tried to think of an excuse to ring the bell again, possibly to get a glimpse inside, if it did turn out that Groen's friend had been left behind by himself. In the end she'd decided to ask whomever was inside for a postage stamp. She'd knocked on the door and called out Mr. Groen's name.

There was no answer.

She put her ear to the door. Then she tiptoed back to her own apartment, fetched her keys, stepped back into the corridor, and slammed her door shut a little too loudly. Next she put her ear to her neighbor's door again. It didn't take long for her to hear someone in there speaking quietly, without receiving an answer. "Who's he talking to now? What on earth?"

A few minutes later she heard the elevator zooming back up. As quickly and quietly as she could, she slipped back inside her own apartment and carefully shut the door behind her. To her chagrin she couldn't see the elevator through her peephole. Perspiring heavily, she stood there, listening.

The elevator door slid open.

She heard the woman ask, "Do you have any diapers?"

There was no reply besides a soft sputter.

The neighbor's front door opened and shut again.

63

Maartje stared blankly at her husband standing in front of her with a cup of tea and a cookie, which he'd added out of habit.

"Maartje, sweetheart, you *must* eat and drink something." Gently he took her by the arm. "Darling, you really have to drink something."

"Yes," she said vacantly. She took the cup and put it down on the table.

The doctor had given her so much sedative that she was barely responsive.

The phone rang. The policeman turned on his recording machine and nodded at Johan to indicate he should answer it.

"Verbeek here, who is this?"

He nodded once or twice.

"What do you think it means?"

Again he listened for a moment.

"Thank you very much, Mr. . . . uh, officer."

191

He replaced the receiver, took a deep breath, and grabbed his wife's shoulders firmly in both hands.

"Listen, Maartje, there's been another call to the school. It was a lady this time. She said Sabine was fine and would probably be returned this evening or tomorrow morning. And that we shouldn't worry."

"That's what they said last time too," said Maartje lifelessly.

"Yes, but this time it was a woman. I don't know why, but it feels more credible. They thought, from the accent, that she might be Surinamese."

"Do you have any friends or acquaintances from Suriname?" the detective at the recording machine interrupted.

The father thought it over and then shook his head.

"No, I don't know any foreigners, really. Except for our Turkish neighbor." Then something occurred to him. "And two Poles. The carpenters who fixed up the baby's room for us."

64

Noon—Town Hall

The mayor wasn't happy with the report from the chief of police. "We're not making much headway, Wiebe, are we? What am I supposed to tell the press?"

"Nothing."

"I can't tell them nothing. I'll be vilified."

"Then just try telling them once again that in the interest of the investigation we have no comment. That's a line everyone's familiar with, anyway."

"I think you may have been listening a little too much to your colleague Stork. I detect a smidgen of sarcasm on your part."

"He's not my colleague and it isn't sarcasm, it's the only thing I can come up with."

"What about those phoned-in tips, how many did you say you received?"

"I don't know the exact number as of this moment, but it must be thirty max."

"So if I say the police are busy following up on dozens of tips, isn't that the truth?"

"Yes, strictly speaking, although we aren't taking any of them very seriously."

"We take everything seriously, Graven; we always say we do anyway."

Graven was silent. He preferred to avoid arguing with her any further; it saved him precious energy.

"Fine, so I'll say we've been collecting tips, and that . . . how many officers are on the case now?"

"Twenty-five."

"Can't I make it forty?"

"Yes, you can, but it isn't true."

"Then I'll say 'close to forty.' "

Graven gazed outside. He thought he should pray for an earthquake or something.

65

Stork carefully went down the list of twenty-seven tips.

Tip 18.
20:26 Hrs. Call from Mr. Schoonderwalt. Unlisted number. Saw a baby carriage in a ditch near his home. Officers Herdegang and Al Achrouir went to investigate and pulled a rusted shopping cart out of the water.

Mathieu Stork shook his head.

Tip 19.
20:44 Hrs. Anonymous caller, probably elderly, male, 068-823-8637. Said his neighbor recently bought a big supply of Pampers. Further questioning reveals said neighbor has "approximately" four little kids. He didn't know how many exactly. At least two very young ones. No action taken.

Tip 20.

21:49 Hrs. Call from a Mrs. van Duivenbode, 225 Vermeer Street. She says her neighbor, in his seventies, has been acting strangely. She thinks she "may" have heard a baby crying. No action taken yet. Should someone be sent to investigate?

Stork studied a map of the city he had unfolded on the desktop.

A detective had traced two circles around the school with a compass. The circles represented the department's estimate of the minimum and maximum distances they thought the kidnapper could have gone on foot.

A third and fourth circle were drawn around the bicycle tunnel where the melee with the teens had taken place. Those circles too corresponded to estimates of the distance a person could cover on foot in five or ten minutes respectively.

Finally there were circles drawn around the spots where, according to the phone company, the calls had originated claiming the baby would be returned.

Stork looked up Vermeer Street on the map. He nodded his head once or twice.

"Could be a coincidence. Could be."

He decided to read the seven remaining tips first. A few minutes later an officer came in with a note in his hand.

"Where's Braspenning?"

"He's gone to get lunch. I'm manning the fort. Why?"

"Another tip's come in."

"Leave it here. Braspenning will be back in fifteen minutes, I'll give it to him."

The officer thanked him and left.

The note read:

11:55 Hrs. Mrs. van Duivenbode called again for the third time. Now says she's sure she heard a baby crying at Number 227, her elderly next-door neighbor's. Seems significant. Move on this? 225 Vermeer Street.

There was a phone number.

Stork sat back, pondering.

He jumped when Braspenning knocked on the door of his own office, poked his head inside, and asked if he could go back to work.

"Go have another coffee. I'll be done here in ten minutes."

"I don't want any coffee."

"Tea, then."

"Fine, Mr. Stork." He shut the door again.

Stork hesitated, then typed in the new tip as number 28 on Braspenning's list. He revised a few more items on the list, jotted down a few things in a note to himself, and stuck it in his pocket. His next move depended on what the mayor was planning to do.

He was expected at a 1:15 crisis meeting with the mayor and police chief to prepare for the press conference.

66

Harry had nodded off on a chair in a corner of the office, and was startled awake.

"Huh?"

"If you'd be so kind as to make another pot of coffee," Hetty Schutter said sharply. Sighing, he got up and went to his kitchenette, which had now been vacated by the police. He put a few less scoops of coffee into the brew basket than usual.

As he returned with the coffee pot, the chairman, Mr. De Visser, was holding forth.

"The first kidnapper calls the school. Makes sense, because that's where he took the baby in the first place. But the second kidnapper calls the parents. That's strange. Whether or not kidnapper number two has the baby, how did he get the parents' phone number?"

"From the phone book, perhaps?" suggested the social worker, who was still living in the White Pages era.

"But you'd need a name. How'd that kidnapper find out their name?"

De Visser looked around the circle. "Did any of you happen to let slip the name Verbeek after the baby was taken?"

They all earnestly shook their heads.

"Fresh pot of coffee," said Harry, just a little too loudly. He'd meant it as a way to change the subject but had managed to draw attention to himself instead.

"You didn't tell anyone the baby's name either, did you?"

Harry felt his blood pressure mounting as he pretended to think. "Hmm...no, not as far as I'm aware."

"Not as far as you're aware?" asked De Visser.

"No, not as far as I'm aware."

Hetty Schutter narrowed her eyes briefly as she gazed at Harry.

De Visser turned to the police psychologist. "What do you think, wouldn't the police have thought of the same thing?"

"Of that I can't be sure," the policeman answered.

67

The mayor arrived at 1:18. She was always a few minutes late. She thought being on time, or even a little early, would give the impression she wasn't very busy. For that reason, she'd sometimes dawdle for a few minutes in her office before bustling out the door.

Stork and Graven were already waiting.

"Good afternoon," they said in unison.

Simone Schaarsberg Donk nodded with something resembling a smile.

"Any news?"

Chief Graven nodded. "Another phone call. A woman this time, probably Surinamese or from the Antilles. She called the school to say the baby would be returned either tonight or tomorrow morning. And we have also pinned down the neighborhood where we believe the suspect lives."

"How wide an area?" asked the mayor.

Graven pointed out a circle drawn on a map of the city within which the streets were highlighted in yellow.

"We think there's a good chance the suspect lives inside this radius."

"How many men and women do you need to comb the area?" The mayor seemed to grow even more brisk than usual. Here, finally, was something calling for action!

"I think...maybe a hundred, but"—the chief picked thoughtfully at his mustache—"the question is: Is that sensible?"

"What do you mean?" asked the mayor.

"Well, I thought we'd already discussed this, but shouldn't we wait until tomorrow morning? To give the kidnapper or kidnappers the chance to park the baby quietly somewhere?"

"And allow them to get away with it? Absolutely not," snapped the mayor. "Besides, it's high time for us to show we're *doing* something."

"Dear Simone, may I say something?" asked Stork.

She wished she could say, "*I'm not your dear Simone*," but she kept her irritation to herself. "Sure, let's hear what you have to say, Mathieu," she said icily.

"I agree with Wiebe. I believe the baby will make its way back home on its own. And with a bit of luck you'll be handed your fake kidnapper on a platter to boot. A house-to-house search of an entire neighborhood now, with a show of force, is only asking for trouble. I'm prepared to take responsibility for postponing any action."

"Except that that isn't in any way your responsibility. It is mine. I think we have to project that we're *doing* something. And we have to assure our citizens their leaders have the guts to take their responsibility seriously."

Stork said nothing. He just stared at her coolly.

"Spare me the condescending looks, Mathieu. You just have to accept a difference of opinion occasionally."

Graven twisted one end of his mustache into a point for a change, but said nothing.

"When's the soonest you can get that area searched, Wiebe?" The mayor had decided to take no more notice of her companions' opinions. This was going to be her chance to shine.

Graven gave it some thought, then shook his head slowly. "Tomorrow morning, at the earliest."

"How early?"

"I don't know, around seven?"

"Most people are still asleep at seven," Stork remarked.

"But that means they're all still at home too," Schaarsberg Donk said with a snooty smile.

"Grandpas and babies are likely to still be home at nine, too."

"I'd prefer to play it safe, but to meet you halfway, let's say eight o'clock." The mayor acted as if it was a great concession on her part.

"And what if I don't go along with this?" asked Stork.

"Then I'll take you off the case at once."

"You can't take me off the case, Simone. You don't have the authority to do so."

They glared at each other in silence.

"Strictly speaking you're right. But I might consider calling the minister."

"Your buddy the minister?"

Schaarsberg Donk nodded.

Stork tried to exchange a look with Graven, but the police chief purposefully looked the other way.

There was an icy silence for at least a minute.

"So then we are agreed. We'll have the police fan out into the neighborhood tomorrow at eight a.m.," said Schaarsberg Donk finally.

"Well, we are not agreed," said Stork. "Let's just agree that it's your decision."

Simone Schaarsberg Donk nodded. "So noted."

68

3:00 p.m.—City Sanitation Department

Wil looked at his watch. It was three o'clock on the dot. At a snail's pace of twelve miles per hour, he drove to the end of the street and turned right. He could drive this route with his eyes closed, after eighteen years as a sanitation worker, the last eight in the same department, on the same vehicle and the same three routes. Wil did not like change. There wasn't much he did like, in fact, except for cars, soccer, beer, and money. A manageable set of priorities, he thought. He also liked television, but only shows about soccer or cars, and he always allowed himself a beer while watching the box. And now, for the first time in his life, he could smell…money. Yesterday he was still thinking in terms of ten-euro bills; today it was in terms of thousands.

It's being tossed into my lap, he thought to himself, *and I'd be mad not to take it.*

Loud honking behind him made him jump; glancing in his rearview mirror, he saw that he was causing a modest traffic jam behind him. Out of habit he gave them the finger, but he pulled his old Toyota aside to let them pass anyway.

This is no good. Driving the entire route at garbage-truck speed attracts too much attention, he said to himself. After some thought, he decided to increase his speed to twenty-five miles per hour, but then he'd have to multiply by two the time he'd clocked. He paused at each trashcan he'd have to empty for the length of time it would normally take. Then he made a note of the time and pulled out again. At two of the trash-cans, he got out of the car as if to stretch his legs, glancing around as surreptitiously as possible. In the end he decided on a can located near the end of his regular route. He estimated the time he'd need to get back to the sanitation garage from there, jotting down all the times on a piece of paper. For a few minutes he sat there intently trying to figure it all out, but finally he just wrote down: "*10:30 Breitner Street, corner of Toorop Street*," and underlined it. Slowly he nodded: That was it. He estimated the distance between Van Tellegen Street and the designated garbage can. Then he guessed how long it would take father Verbeek to ride his bike there: fifteen minutes. Brilliant, that, telling him to come by bike, Wil decided. The cops probably wouldn't have thought of that. A bike was harder to keep tabs on than a pedestrian or a car. So he'd have to make the call at around ten fifteen, while his partner was occupied emptying trashcans.

He started the engine, drove to the shopping mall, chose one of the six telephone stores enhancing the mall's shopping ambiance, and bought the cheapest prepaid phone he could find, with a €10 credit. He was already sorry he'd have to ditch it in a canal the next day. *Oh, stop complaining, Staff, remember the bag of moolah you'll have instead.* Wil didn't much like talking to people, but he made an exception when it came to talking to himself.

Next he drove to the supermarket, bought a six-pack, and drove home. There he found that his wife, as he'd expected, had consumed the last beer, and he gave himself a pat on the back for his foresight. He made a great show of cracking open the first of his beers right under his wife's nose, then turned on the TV. To her astonishment, he switched to the news instead of his usual sports channel.

69

Jenny put on her coat. She was going home at her usual hour, though she hadn't gotten around to ironing my shirts or mopping the floors. Instead she had bathed the baby in the sink, wrapped a sprained ankle, and given two old men a slightly more optimistic outlook on life.

In between she'd also done the laundry and made tea.

I was really touched to receive so much help at such a difficult time, especially as it was offered with unconditional kindness.

"Jennifer, thank you so much for everything, no matter what happens next."

"You're very welcome, Mr. Groen, I'm happy to do it for you and your friend."

"Well, we'll see you in the morning, then, at eight thirty."

"Don't forget to give the little darling a bottle at seven, won't you, and change her diaper. I'd like to set out with a clean baby."

I nodded. Evert, from the couch, put up his hand and attempted something that looked like a grin.

Jenny waved back merrily, then shut the door behind her.

"Great woman, that, Henk. Wouldn't mind having her come clean my place."

"Yes, she's a treasure. Aside from her cleaning skills, even. She doesn't get on your nerves."

"And smart, and practical too," Evert went on. "With a bit of luck, at nine thirty tomorrow we'll be popping the champagne."

"Let's run through it again," I said. "She'll be here at eight thirty, with a baby basket. We'll have given our little girl a bottle and a diaper change; we'll dress her warmly, give her a last cuddle, and then tuck her in the basket and take her downstairs. All without making a sound, so as not to wake the woman next door. Jennifer straps the basket into the car and drives to Heerenplein Square. There she'll leave the baby inside the community center, to which her cousin has a key. There's never anyone around early in the morning, so she should be able to go in without anyone noticing. If necessary she'll drive around the block a couple of times first, if she's worried about being seen. Then she'll drive home. If everything goes according to plan, and Christine gets left there safe and sound, Jenny will call from the car to tell me. Then I'll walk to the phone booth and call the school. If there's no one to pick up again, I'll call 911. The baby is found and returned to the parents. All's well that ends well. Are we missing anything important?"

We both went over the scenario again in our minds.

"Jenny should wear something different when she takes

Christina. Old clothes that she can throw in the garbage afterward. And glasses. She should disguise herself, go incognito."

"Should she?" I decided to phone her later to suggest it.

"And then, by nine thirty or sooner, it's all over, and we can break out the bubbly. I'll get nice and hammered, and then I'll take a cab to the ER."

"Maybe it's best if you get there sober," I suggested, "that makes a better impression. After the ER you'll take a taxi back here, and *then* we'll both get nice and hammered, to celebrate the happy outcome. Okay?"

"Okay. Oh, and around ten tomorrow, while I'm in the ER, could you let Mo out again for me?"

"Of course, pal. But first we have another long night ahead of us. I don't think I'll get much sleep again, I'm too nervous."

"Haven't you got any pills?" asked Evert.

"Pills?"

"Yeah, sleeping pills."

"No, I've never needed them."

70

Harry wasn't in the best of shape. After a long, wretched evening at the school, then a sleepless night, and then another full day at work, he was looking drawn and pale, with bags under his eyes and a two-day beard. He had begged, almost pleaded with Hetty to let him go home. The principal, realizing that Harry, as a representative of the school, made a rather disheveled impression, finally gave him permission.

"Be back here tomorrow at eight, please. And change your clothes, Har," she had added sweetly.

Now he was sitting in his armchair at home, fretting.

His wife had given him a cup of tea and was peeling potatoes.

To tell the truth, Harry was flipping out. He didn't even feel like having a beer. And the potato chips that accompanied his tea tasted like cardboard.

The thing bothering him had to do with his brother.

He kept coming back to the chairman's question: Had he

given anyone the kidnapped baby's address? To make matters worse, he'd overheard someone at the police station say the kidnapper who'd asked for a ransom spoke with a broad Amsterdam accent.

He wasn't sure, but he might have told his brother Wil the name of the parents and where they lived. And Wil's Amsterdam accent was as broad as could be.

Was Wil capable of planning such a thing? Harry wondered for the umpteenth time. And then would he follow through on it too?

For the umpteenth time, the answer was yes and yes. Harry might not always be 100 percent square, but Wil was a rotten apple, plain and simple. And a pretty stupid rotten apple too. Not that Harry thought of himself as such a paragon of virtue, but at least he almost always knew how to stay out of a sticky situation. Whereas Wil had had quite a few brushes with the law in his time. Slugfest here, community service there.

So would Wil and his Neanderthal brain be trying to cash in on this? Harry asked himself the question and promptly came up with the answer: Wil could have decided that, with the information Harry had given him, he could try demanding a ransom without running much of a risk.

Harry shook his head.

"What are you shaking your head for?" asked his wife.

"Nothing. I think I'll go see Wil in a bit."

She stared at him in surprise. "What in the world do you want with that idiot?" she asked after a short silence.

"Hey, hey, that idiot *is* my brother, remember."

"Well, congratulations for having a brother like that one. I'm not coming, anyway. I've had it with that bonehead. And his wife too."

"As you like." Harry was glad enough not to have to think of an excuse not to let her come.

71

"What's up with you? Sit down, man, can't you! You look as if you've got ants in your pants!"

Wil burped. "Just listen to me for once, woman. I got problems, you don't even wanna know."

"That's exactly what I *do* want to know, Wil."

"The problem is, you're always trying to stick your nose in my business. There's some things you shouldn't wanna know."

"I'll decide if I do." Peevishly his wife put on her headphones and a few seconds later was absorbed in a rerun of her favorite soap.

She might not be the brightest bulb in the box, but she could do the math. And besides, she knew exactly how much he made. How was he supposed to explain to her the hundred thousand bucks coming his way? She'd nag him to death trying to worm it out of him, and there were very few men who wouldn't crumble under that sort of pressure.

He had a few options. He could spend the money extremely frugally. Or he could make up something about the lottery. Or he could tell her the truth.

He rejected the last one first. He had no idea, really, how she'd react if he told her how he'd come into the moolah. Maybe she'd be proud. Or scared. Or she'd want to give the money back, though he reckoned that was unlikely. Anyway, she was probably incapable of keeping her big mouth shut, and she would tell her sister. And in that case, he might as well print it in the newspaper.

The idea of spending the cash in small increments didn't appeal to him either. Even if every week he spent, let's say, a hundred euros more than usual, she was bound to notice. And if he spent just fifty more a week, it would take him two thousand weeks to get through it all. He didn't bother to work it out exactly, but he knew he'd be in his grave before all the money was gone.

He had to think of some kind of prize he could win, without making her suspicious. A raffle or something. But then of course she'd want to see the winning ticket, which he didn't have.

"Shit, it ain't easy," he muttered to himself.

"What ain't easy?" came her voice from the easy chair beside him.

Wil, startled, turned to look at her. How could she have heard him with her headphones on?

72

The mayor would have liked to put three squads of riot police on the job, but then Stork and Graven would both have refused to have anything to do with it. They had also managed to nix her idea of sending in armed SWAT teams. She'd been persuaded to change her mind by the chief of the national prosecutor's office, in a phone call arranged by Stork. A door-to-door search was to be conducted by detectives and plainclothes officers divided into four-man teams, assigned to check out forty addresses each.

The relationship between Stork and Mayor Schaarsberg Donk hadn't exactly improved. "Icy" was a nice way of putting it. They had not said goodbye when they'd parted at the town hall. Graven tried to stay as neutral as possible, but in the end he chose Stork as the lesser of two evils. You wouldn't really call them friends either, but at least Stork showed common sense in choosing to tamp things down. He thought Schaarsberg Donk had completely lost her mind in trying to look strong by putting on a show of force.

Patches of sweat were slowly but surely blooming on the chief's jacket. He had a pounding headache. The blister pack of Tylenol he'd brought with him from home that morning was now empty, and he wasn't going to have a chance to ask his secretary discreetly to get him some more.

Technology had once again failed the police in their hour of need. The big digital display on the wall that was supposed to let Graven pull up maps was on the fritz. The IT department, currently consisting of one technician, had gone home two hours before and turned off his phone.

Graven stood in front of a large paper map of the city fixed to the digital board with Scotch tape, and he was using a ruler as a pointer.

Twenty plainclothes officers watched in silence, jotting down street names and timeframes. There was some debate on what order made the most sense for tackling the street searches. Graven cut the discussion short. "It doesn't really matter where we start. I'm not expecting to see a high-speed chase all around the city to catch an old geezer pushing a baby carriage!"

Next, instructions were given as to how the officers should proceed. Ring the doorbell, identify themselves, explain what they were looking for, and ask if they could come in for a bit. If they were refused, insist and explain that a search warrant was on the way.

"I hope you don't get any residents who are informed enough to know it doesn't work that way," Stork remarked.

"'On the way' is a relative term, Mathieu," Graven said. "I don't think there's anything unlawful about putting it like that."

"You just go ahead and do your thing, Wiebe."

Finally they ran down the logistics: who would be in which team, which cars to put in service, methods of communication, and who was responsible for what.

Everyone was to reassemble at six the next morning at HQ.

Stork said goodbye and went into his own office to think. After a while he made his way to Bram Braspenning's office, emerging ten minutes later. He'd left a short handwritten note on the desk, which Bram would discover at 7:00 a.m.; Bram had never in twenty years arrived late for work.

Then Stork called his wife on his personal phone.

"I'll be home in fifteen minutes. I have something to discuss with you."

"Something serious?"

"Something...how should I put it...something fun."

"Something fun? I'm always ready for fun, darling, you know that."

73

Two and a Half Hours Earlier—Wil's Apartment

"Who there?" Wil shouted into the intercom.

"It's me, Harry."

There was a pause. "What the f— are you doing here?"

"I've got to talk to you. Are you alone?"

"No, Ans is here. Why?"

"It's best if she doesn't hear what we have to talk about."

There was another pause.

"I'm coming down with the dog," said Wil, who went back into the living room.

"What was that?" asked his wife.

"Dude from the power company. I've had it with all those bozos trying to sell you something. I feel like getting some fresh air. I'll take the dog out for a walk."

"Huh? Don't you want to wait until after dinner?"

"No, I'm not waiting until after dinner."

His wife looked after him as he stepped into the corridor and called the dog. She thought he'd been acting weird lately.

★ ★ ★

Downstairs Wil greeted his brother gruffly. Together they walked to a narrow strip of grass already littered with dog shit.

Wil let the dog off the leash and turned to Harry. "What do you want with me?"

Harry hesitated, then came out with it. "I think you've got something to do with the ransom demand for that baby."

"How in hell did you know that?" Wil was so astonished that he completely forgot to deny it.

"So it's true?"

Wil realized he'd acted like a four-year-old. "No, of course not. I'm just surprised."

"If I get wind of the fact that you have something to do with it, I'll rat you out. Unless you tell me right now what you've got up your sleeve."

Wil thought it over.

He looked at his dog, crouched amid the litter, its back bowed and quivering, squeezing out a turd.

"Okay," he then said quietly.

★ ★ ★

Fifteen minutes later they said goodbye on the sidewalk in front of Wil's building. Harry promised to keep his mouth shut in return for fifteen thousand euros. Not a bad deal, really. He decided it was unlikely they'd ever be able to pin anything on him. He was going to buy a new RV with it.

The brothers had also agreed not to contact each other for the foreseeable future.

74

"Not a smidgen of empathy. No sense of principle. All she cares about is herself and her own image. Makes me sick."

Mathieu Stork was venting his spleen about the mayor. Rita, his wife, had put her arm around him and patiently listened to a lengthy account of what had happened at the school and town hall. She agreed with her husband's analysis of the situation. Some old guy had probably snatched the baby carriage in an unpremeditated impulse, and returning the child safely to the parents without being detected seemed to be giving him considerable trouble. Maybe he was terrified of being sent to jail, and if not, he'd definitely be dreading the inevitable hullaballoo resulting from his heist. If this granddad were outed as the kidnapper of little baby Jesus, he could kiss his days of venturing out into public goodbye; he'd be eaten alive.

75

Wil started on his second family-size bag of paprika potato chips. His wife looked at him askance.

"Enjoying yourself?" she asked. "That's your second bag."

Wil was startled from his musings. "Yeah, I'm enjoying myself, can't you see, as long as I don't have to listen to you nagging the hell outta me."

"I'm not nagging you."

He stared at her scornfully and decided to ignore her.

You've got more important things to worry about, he said to himself.

He wasn't happy about his brother unexpectedly sticking his nose in. Because, one, it was going to cost him fifteen thousand bucks; and, two, because he thought the more people who knew about his plan, the more likely it was something would go wrong. For a moment he considered throwing in the towel, but no—for the first time in his life he could smell real money, and he wasn't going to let his moron of a brother rob him of that. He did realize, though, that it meant being tied to him for the rest of his life.

"Maybe he'll even come in handy one of these days."

"Who'll come in handy?" asked his wife.

"Nothing."

Thursday, December 23

76

Chief of Police Graven found himself gulping down a handful of Tylenol a day; to make matters worse, he'd cut himself
twice that morning shaving. Two pinkish wisps of cotton
wool marked the spots. Chief Prosecutor Stork wasn't in much
better shape, with a three-day stubble and eyes red from exhaustion. The mayor was the only one who looked polished, as
if ready to strut the runway in a fashion show for middle-aged
women, in a neat suit, discreet makeup, and a sleek hairdo.

She was having Graven talk her through the plans that
had been drawn up for the precinct search. Stork stood
by, silent.

Meanwhile some forty detectives were preparing themselves to go out on the job. They'd been divided into ten
teams, each assigned to a different section of the area. They
were to go door to door, asking for an old man and a baby.

There was a knock on the door of the mayor's office.
Braspenning appeared in the doorway. The three others
looked up.

"Spit it out, Bram," said Graven, with an expression that showed little confidence.

Bram began stuttering nervously. "I, uh...I just...just went over the tips again...uh.. and I think there may be something we should look into there."

"And you couldn't have told us about it sooner?" the mayor said, irritated.

Graven ignored her. "Speak up, Bram, what have you found that no one's noticed?"

"Well, uh, we only just finished working on all the tips, and it turns out one lady called in several times about hearing a baby in the apartment of her neighbor, an old man. And she lives on a street that fits."

"Fits how?" asked Stork.

"It's right in the area we've been looking at. Vermeer Street. Number 227."

"And why are you only coming to us with this now?" Schaarsberg Donk pressed him.

"We just finished the list, ma'am. A colleague asked me to look into it."

Bram Braspenning, whose parents had saddled him with a name of unfortunate alliteration, proceeded to give a rundown of all the tips that had come in. Verbatim, and by heart. They couldn't help but be impressed.

"Good work, Bram. Thanks. Stay close in case we need you," Graven complimented him, then went on, "I don't think there's much doubt. What do we do now? We'll have to rethink the whole situation." The chief looked at the mayor.

She considered briefly, then said, "We raid the place."

"Ho, ho, let's think it over calmly first," Stork proposed, "and in the meantime, let's call off the door-to-door search for now."

"It's true that a raid on a building and a door-to-door search of the neighborhood are kind of counterproductive, Simone," Graven said, backing him up.

The mayor hesitated. "Okay, then I propose we dispatch a SWAT team to the address at once."

"Or perhaps two female officers? So as not to alarm anyone?" Stork suggested.

"No way, Mathieu. If they botch it we'll be the laughing stock of the entire nation. We're tackling this *my* way, with a full SWAT team. Do you have one ready to go, Wiebe?"

"They'll be ready to leave in fifteen minutes."

"With no search warrant or preparation to speak of?" Stork objected.

"There's nothing to prepare and there's no time to do it."

"That sounds like a contradiction, Simone."

"I've just about had it with your meddling, Mathieu. We're going to show we mean business now. With any luck, Baby Jesus will be back in her parents' arms less than an hour from now."

"And then I'm sure you will be..." Stork didn't finish his sentence.

"What am I sure to be?" asked the mayor sharply.

"The first to be photographed with the parents, for the newspapers."

Mayor Schaarsberg Donk glared at him. "If that helps to give the citizens of this city some reassurance, then that is definitely what I'll do."

77

Half an Hour Earlier—Wil's Apartment

The alarm went off at six thirty, but Wil was already awake. He'd hardly slept a wink. He got out of bed as stealthily as he could so as not to wake his wife.

"Jesus, did you have ants in your pants last night? You never stopped tossing and turning!" came a hoarse voice beside him.

"I'm not Jesus."

"Oh, go to hell."

By six fifty Wil was out the door. He couldn't get a thing down, only a cup of tea. His hands shook so badly he had trouble getting his key into the car lock.

At seven thirty on the nose he parked his car and a minute later ambled into the sanitation canteen. He'd been driving around the block for thirty minutes so he wouldn't get to work early.

A dozen or so co-workers were already there, but none of them were in the mood to say good morning this early in the day. Wil served himself a coffee from the coffee machine and went looking for Schepper. He found him sitting in his usual corner, reading *De Telegraaf*. Wil growled something incoherent. Schepper, mocking him, growled back for a long nonsensical minute. It was the same thing every morning.

Two minutes later Wil stood up. "Let's go."

Schepper stared at him in surprise. "Are you feeling sick or something, or are you just off your rocker?"

"Why?"

"In the ten years I've known you, you've never been the first to get going."

Wil realized he was indeed acting differently than normal, and he sat back down. He was a wreck. At seven forty-five on the dot the boss walked in.

"Mornin', gentlemen. Let's get to work please. Have a good day."

Wil got up slowly. He was trying to act as normal as possible.

"Something wrong with you, Staff?" It was Schepper.

"What now?" Wil exclaimed, squealing as if he'd just sat down on a thumbtack.

"What, what now? You didn't drink your coffee and you haven't said a word of complaint about anything."

"I've got a splitting headache."

"Well then, take a sick day. You've only been out sick six times this year."

"Shut the fuck up."

"Ah, that sounds more like the Wil I know."

Wil took the keys to garbage truck 23 from the wall and strode into the garage. Schepper followed behind, chuckling. "You're even walking faster than usual."

Wil growled something and slowed down. *Calm down! Calm the fuck down, you oaf*, he cursed to himself.

They climbed into their truck. Engine on, heat on, radio on. Wil pulled into the street slowly, heading for the first trashcan on their route.

He'd worked out that the twenty-seventh can was the one.

78

6:45 a.m.—Princess Margriet School

Harry took a sip of his coffee. He'd arrived at school extra early, so that he'd have the place all to himself for a while. The police had withdrawn from the school; the DO NOT CROSS tapes lay crumpled in the wastepaper basket. The reporters were gone too, the children and teachers were on Christmas break, and Hetty the principal had called to say she had a board meeting at nine and wouldn't be there until around twelve.

Harry had not slept well. In the middle of the night he'd woken up in a sweat, as it had suddenly occurred to him that if they caught his brother with the ransom money, the trail would inevitably lead to him.

He'd tossed and turned the rest of the night, wondering what he should say to the police if that happened. He hadn't come up with anything. Harry was quite sure that if his brother was caught, he would try to pin most of the blame on Harry. The fact that Wil would definitely have done the same even if Harry hadn't gone to him and demanded a cut was scant consolation. Now, with a bit of luck, he'd at least get a new RV out of it.

He sighed and took another sip. His coffee had gone cold.

79

Mayor Schaarsberg Donk would have liked nothing better than to send in an anti-terrorist squad armed with AK-47s to break into the apartment, but she'd let herself be persuaded by Graven that that was overdoing it a bit and might scare off the kidnappers. Instead, six plainclothes detectives, each armed with a concealed pistol and bulletproof vest, were now lurking in three positions near the building's entrance.

Two other cops, hidden in the woods in back of the building, were watching the seventh-floor balcony, just in case someone took it into his head to sneak out that way.

A female detective was hovering close to the entrance, waiting for one of the residents to come out and release the door lock. An elderly lady with a little dog stepped out of the elevator and pressed the automatic door opener. The officer went up to her and flashed her badge. The old lady, apologizing, fumbled in her handbag for her reading glasses in order to inspect said badge. Meanwhile the five other detectives had run up and pushed their way unceremoniously into the front hall. The little dog started barking, yanking at its lead. One of the officers tried hustling dog and owner outside, finally succeeding with only a minor rip in his pants. The lady, dumbstruck, found herself standing outside the door, her little dog yapping furiously all the while. A lone passerby wondered what all the fuss was about.

Two of the cops ran up the stairs, while the other four took the elevator. The elevator door slid open on the seventh floor. While waiting for their colleagues to make it up the stairs, two officers posted themselves stealthily on either side of door number 227. The other two stood ready with a heavy block of wood to break down the door. The last two officers finally arrived, and one of the cops by the door mimed the countdown on his fingers: *three, two, one, NOW*.

The door gave way with a great crash. The cops who'd been posted on either side of the door stormed inside, pistols drawn. The front hall was empty. On to the living room. No one in there, except for a cat. The kitchen was empty as well. It was a rather preposterous sight: six hulking armed cops in the tidy little apartment of a respectable senior citizen.

All that was left was the bedroom. They threw the door open. The light fell onto an old man's striped pajamas. Above them, a startled face. Eyes wide open, disheveled wisps of gray hair. Mouth open in astonishment. The cops were no less flummoxed.

The resident of number 227 was the first to recover.

"Good morning, gentlemen, madam, can I help you? Are you looking for something?"

An inspired question, given the circumstances.

80

"May I offer you a cup of coffee, or would you prefer to search the apartment first?" That's what I'd have liked to say, but I thought it might be pushing things a bit. Instead I asked for permission to get out of bed, and politely inquired what was the reason for their visit.

The man who'd burst in first appeared to be the group's commander. He explained they were looking for a baby but that they'd "possibly" been mistaken.

I assured them they had indeed been mistaken, because there had never been a baby in my apartment. Then I asked the officers opening and closing all the closet and wardrobe doors if they had checked under the bed yet.

It did occur to me, although a bit late, that I shouldn't act *too* helpful. I was better off sticking to honest bewilderment.

"What makes you think there's a baby in here anyway? And why does that justify a police raid?" I sputtered.

"Your neighbor..." an officer standing next to the chief

235

began, but he got no further, since one glare from his boss told him to shut up.

"Oh, my neighbor . . . yes, well, she's . . . how shall we say . . . a bit confused sometimes," I said as compassionately as I could. "You should take anything she has to say with a grain of salt. She's very lonely, you see."

With a curt nod, the chief sent two of his detectives to the apartment next door, and a short while later I heard her insist in a shaky little voice that she really had heard a baby, and that several "strange" people had visited me, including another old man.

The chief was called away, probably for a confab. Five minutes later he was back.

"Your neighbor insists that you had an elderly gentleman in here yesterday, and a dark-skinned lady. Is that right?"

"Certainly. The lady is my cleaner, and the gentleman was someone from the church."

"Someone from the church?"

"Yes, I haven't been religious for many years, but every so often someone will stop by to try to talk me into believing in the existence of a merciful God. I always offer them a cup of tea, and hope they won't stay too long."

"Your neighbor said it was a friend of yours."

"No, trust me, I'd never seen the good man before."

The officer asked for their names. I gave him the name and phone number of my cleaning lady, and told him that all I knew about the church fellow was that his name was Anton and he was from Utrecht. That seemed to be enough for my interrogator. Another cop returned to tell him in a whisper they hadn't found anything.

"No trace? No dirty diaper, baby clothes, formula?" his superior whispered back. I think he must have hoped I was a bit deaf.

"No, nothing at all."

The chief now turned back to me and began excusing himself to me profusely. It was probably just an unfortunate misunderstanding. He would send someone as soon as possible to repair the damage to the front door. He also offered at least three times to arrange victim assistance for me.

I politely turned him down three times in return.

"I'll try to recover from the shock on my own," I said, "and I assume that you are capable of seeing yourselves out." I nodded toward the splintered door.

The officers shuffled backward out the door. The last one tried to pull it shut behind him, but without success. Twice it spontaneously swung open again, and finally the officer just left it that way.

I briefly considered ringing the neighbor's doorbell right then and there and pretending to be interested in hearing her story, but I was wiped from all the stress and excitement. I sank into my easy chair and didn't leave it for a good long while.

81

Eleven Hours Earlier—Hendrik's Building

Rita Stork strode along at a purposeful pace. Turning the corner, she found herself on Vermeer Street. She was a bit nervous, but pleasantly so. She felt honored that her husband had recruited her for this undercover operation. Mathieu and Rita had agreed: They would try to steer the course of events ever so slightly in the kidnapper's favor. A door-to-door search was still always an option if they didn't succeed.

"And if the baby's back in the parents' arms without a big hoo-ha, the mayor's reputation will be just a bit the worse for wear," Mathieu had gleefully concluded.

They did know, of course, that there were considerable risks attached to their scheme. If anyone ever found out that the chief prosecutor had involved his wife in more or less sabotaging a covert police operation, then the aforementioned prosecutor would be out on the street—or even looking at, in his own words, "the penitentiary institution."

Rita had smiled: "Sounds quite grand, actually. I bet some people think 'penitentiary institution' refers to some sort of spa."

Mathieu had asked her twice, "You're sure you want to go through with this?"

She was sure.

Luckily the street was almost deserted. Rita tried reading the names by the doorbells as discreetly as possible.

Seventh floor, number 225, MRS. VAN DUIVENBODE.

That was her, the lady who'd called the police three times. She had two neighbors, presumably, because each floor appeared to have three apartments and three names attached. She hesitated. Should she ring both the neighbors' bells? In the end she decided to stick to the plan she and her husband had come up with: the tactic of surprise.

She perused the names on the other floors. She decided on MRS. R.H. PEERDEMAN and MRS. DE BRUIJN. She pressed one of the bells.

There was a crackling sound, then: "Who's there?"

"Mrs. Peerdeman, it's me, Mrs. De Bruijn, in number 264. I left my keys at home and I can't get in downstairs. Can you please buzz me in?"

There was a brief silence. Mrs. Peerdeman seemed to be hesitating.

"I'm not a stranger, you can let me in." Rita glanced at the names. "I'm the one who lives next door to Mr. Amrani."

Again it was quiet. Then the buzzer went.

"Thanks so much, Mrs. Peerdeman."

"You're welcome, Mrs. De Bruijn."

A smile spread over Rita's face. She loved unlooked-for adventures, and this one was special. She seemed to have landed in a cop show, one in which she even had a major role. The first hurdle had been cleared easily. Now for the next one: to get inside the apartment. She took the elevator to the seventh floor. There were three doors facing the elevator. She read the names on the doors. MRS. VAN DUIVENBODE. That was the one she should avoid. The second one read THE YILMAZ FAMILY. That didn't sound like an old man. The third door wore a neat nameplate: H.G. GROEN. That had to be him. Her heart was pounding. Silently taking a deep breath, she rang the bell.

Nothing happened. She rang again. A few seconds later a key was turned and the door opened just a crack. An eye appeared. Rita proceeded as she had planned: She stared at the eye sternly and put her forefinger emphatically to her lips, at the same time pushing the door with her other hand until the crack was wide enough to slip inside. Shutting the door quickly behind her, she put her hands in the air as if surrendering, again put her finger to her lips, and waved the neat-looking old gentleman who had opened the door into the living room. He seemed quite stunned, and, meek as a sheep, turned for her to follow him.

"Who is it, Henkie?" a male voice asked from the living room.

"To tell you the truth, I have no idea," the first man replied, stepping into the room.

"Allow me to introduce myself," said Rita. "I am Rita, and I've come to help. If, that is, what I suspect is going on here is in fact the case."

"Well, Rita, what is it you suspect, then?" asked the considerably more disheveled-looking man seated on the couch, with one leg resting on an old-fashioned ottoman.

"That you may have taken a baby by accident, and are now encountering some difficulties getting it back to the worried parents."

Two mouths fell open wide in surprise.

Rita couldn't help laughing, then went on: "I'll help you—on condition that you don't ask any questions."

82

8:30 a.m.—Town Hall

Mathieu Stork was doing his very best not to gloat, but he didn't quite manage it. The mayor, for her part, was trying in vain to hide her fury.

"Who did those tips come from, then?"

"From a nosy old neighbor with a little too much imagination," Chief Graven replied.

Stork couldn't help himself. "It might have been better, after all, to send out two female officers to make some inquiries first."

"Yes, Mathieu, in hindsight, in hindsight. And besides," Mayor Schaarsberg Donk continued, "the decision to take decisive action was unanimously agreed on, by the tripartite authority of mayor, police, and chief prosecutor, let that be clear."

Stork stared at her with narrowed eyes.

"To be fair, Simone, it wasn't Mathieu's decision, even if officially the authority was his," Graven unexpectedly backed up his colleague.

"The way the decision was made remains within these four walls. I insist."

Again Stork said nothing but went on staring at her.

"To change the subject," Graven said, "it seems that a reporter has gotten wind of this morning's police action. There may very well be a piece about it this afternoon in the *North Holland Gazette*."

"Even more reason to circle the wagons," said Simone Schaarsberg Donk, "and to call a press conference later this a.m."

"And what about the door-to-door search?" asked Graven.

"That's postponed for now."

Stork couldn't suppress a condescending smile. "What a sensible woman you are, Simone. Want to bet—let's say, a nice bottle of wine—that the baby will be home unharmed by tonight at the latest?"

"I never gamble."

83

8:45 a.m.—The Baby's Parents' House

It was getting light out. Rita, pushing the baby carriage, traversed the park in the direction of Van Tellegen Street. It had been a long time since she'd strolled with a pram, but she had no trouble making it look completely normal. It also helped that there was practically no one out yet. Two blocks from Van Tellegen Street, she stopped. She gave a quick wave to a dark car parked a little way off, then pivoted on her heels, retraced her steps a short way, and turned into a side street. The baby carriage stayed put, next to a lamppost.

Thirty seconds later, some two hundred yards away, the door of a house on Van Tellegen Street flew open wide and out ran Sabine's father and a police officer, with the mother in her bathrobe close behind. Two cars across the street flashed their headlights. The party of three raced around the street corner.

The driver of the parked car saw them coming, started his engine, turned on his headlights, and drove away.

The policeman was the first to reach the baby carriage, and he looked inside. He turned to the parents and raised an arm, jubilant.

"*YESSS!*"

The father tripped, fell, and got up again, made it to the carriage, leaned down, and very carefully picked up a little bundle of blankets topped with a little hat. Tears were running down his face. A few seconds later the mother reached him. Together they held their baby; together they wept.

After two minutes of this the officer asked delicately if they didn't want to go back inside.

"It's a little cold out here, you see."

84

9:00 a.m.—Town Hall

Stork and Graven had both decided to sit down. Simone Schaarsberg Donk was pacing up and down with a phone pressed to her ear.

"No, nothing's been found. But we've had a tip-off that...No...yes, that's right. It seems a reporter has seen something."

She stopped pacing and closed her eyes for a few seconds. Her face looked grim. She shook her head slowly, as if she was still having a hard time believing it.

"We've called the papers to request they keep a lid on any information they may have," she went on.

Graven fiddled with his mustache. Stork looked at his watch.

"That I don't know. It could be that..."

The door opened. An officer stood in the doorway, evidently eager to deliver a message. The mayor, annoyed, raised her eyebrows at him.

"A very urgent call on line three, Madam Mayor."

"Forgive me, it seems there's a new development. Will you excuse me a minute...Fine, I'll call you back shortly."

She put down the receiver and picked up another one.

"Mayor Schaarsberg Donk speaking."

She listened attentively. A look came over her face that was half vexation, half disbelief.

"Thank you."

She turned to look at the chief prosecutor and chief of police. There was a short silence.

"The baby has been found. Delivered on the sly by some unknown person, around the corner of the parents' street."

Graven gave a deep sigh of relief and Stork beamed from ear to ear. They slapped each other on the back. Then Stork turned to the mayor.

"Simone, my dear, you don't seem at all happy. If you go before the press with a sour face like that, it won't do much for your image. Try projecting a little human warmth."

Simone would dearly have liked to rip his tongue out of his mouth, but with considerable difficulty she managed to squeeze out a smile.

"Of course I'm happy. Elated, even. I just have to get used to the idea that we've brought this affair to a satisfactory conclusion."

Across from her two pairs of eyebrows were raised.

Then the police chief indulgently said, "A very satisfactory ending, yes, but...what are we going to do now about the kidnapper demanding a ransom?"

"Arrest him, of course."

"Then we'll have to keep it quiet that the baby's been returned for a little longer," said Graven.

"Fine by me," said Stork with a big grin.

Simone Schaarsberg Donk glanced at him suspiciously.

85

It was touching to see how happy and relieved Maartje and Johan Verbeek were. They took turns holding Sabine, and sometimes they held her together. They radiated happiness. Sabine had soon nodded off, but her mother kept the sleeping little girl on her lap, caressing the little baby hands. Every now and then a tear of happiness came rolling down her cheek.

Maartje was finally in the mood for a cup of tea, and her husband went into the kitchen to make her one.

A few minutes later there was a knock on the door. Johan answered it holding the teapot. Two new detectives stood outside.

"Morning, sir. We'd like to discuss with you how to handle the person demanding the ransom."

In his euphoria Johan hadn't given that wrinkle another moment's thought.

"Oh, of course, please come in. Would you like some tea?"

Once they were seated on the sofa, the elder of the two

said, "You're under no obligation at all, sir. We can use a stand-in. Actually, I'd advise you to take that option, to be honest, after all you've been through. After all, there's no longer a baby in play."

Johan was quick to make up his mind.

"Go for the stand-in. That way I don't risk putting my foot in it either."

He turned to his wife. "Right, Maartje?"

But Maartje was oblivious; she only had eyes for her child.

"That's fine, sir. So—you know you're not supposed to tell anyone for the next few hours that you've got your daughter back?"

Johan looked puzzled.

"But I already have."

"You already have? Didn't anyone tell you to wait?"

"No. But the only people I've called so far are my parents and the in-laws. And the school. I thought... they must be terribly worried over there."

"Who did you speak to?"

"My father."

"No, I mean, at the school."

"A man. He said he'd pass it on."

"Was it the custodian?"

"I don't know."

The detective immediately picked up the phone and called the Princess Margriet School. The line was busy.

86

Harry called his brother for the second time.

"You've reached the van Staverens. We can't come to the phone right now. Leave a message."

Wil never called back, being a bit of a cheapskate. If you wanted to speak with him, *you* had to call *him*, and not the other way around. That's the way it worked, according to Wil.

If you don't pick up right this minute, it'll cost you dearly, you idiot, thought Harry, dialing his brother's number a third time.

"Oh, shit!" he swore, because halfway through dialing it occurred to him his brother wasn't at home, of course, but on the job. He put the phone away and in hindsight was glad his sister-in-law hadn't picked up. He wouldn't have known what to say.

He was frantically trying to think. Unless he managed to reach his brother in time, Wil would be walking straight into the arms of the fuzz the moment he got his hands on the ransom, seeing that the kidnapped baby was no longer missing.

The school telephone rang.

Surely he isn't calling me back on the school's number? Harry thought in a panic. *The police are listening in!*

"Princess Margriet School, van Staveren speaking."

"This is the police. Are you the one who was just contacted by Mr. Verbeek?"

"Uh, yes, that's right, why?"

"What Mr. Verbeek told you regarding the kidnapping must under no circumstances be made public. Which is to say that you can't tell anyone."

"Oh? He didn't say anything about that."

"You haven't told anyone else yet?"

"No, no." And it was true too, Harry realized to his chagrin.

"Nobody?"

"Only the school principal. If I don't call her with that kind of news, I'm fired."

"Would you please call your principal immediately and tell her to not breathe a word about the baby being found?"

"Yes of course, of course."

After a short pause, the officer said goodbye and hung up.

Harry was now a bit frantic. He looked up the number of Wil's place of work in the phone book, found it, and dialed it.

"Sanitation department."

"I need to speak to my brother Wil, Wil van Staveren, it's urgent. A serious illness in the family."

"Mr. van Staveren is out on his route right now."

"Could you please tell me where his route goes?"

87

"Well, that cast sure looks good on you. Wouldn't they let you choose the color?"

"No, it was either white or black."

Jenny was pushing Evert's wheelchair out of the hospital entrance. She patted him on the shoulder.

Next she'll be pinching my cheek, Evert feared.

A watery sun was out; the world had a friendly look about it.

"Where to now, Mr. Evert?"

"To my dog, Mo. He's been waiting for us for ages. The mongrel needs to be let out. Could you possibly..."

"Ho, ho, I'm happy to help, but I'm not walking any dogs. Not my thing."

Evert decided to ask Hendrik to take Mo for another walk later. His pal had promised to drop by at ten thirty, once he'd had a chance to recover from all the excitement.

Jenny stopped the wheelchair next to an ancient Opel, opened the passenger door, and managed—with some pushing and shoving—to get Evert out of the wheelchair and into the car.

"Hey, hey, slow down, my other leg's still outside, that one has to come along too."

Jenny, unperturbed, yanked and prodded until everything was inside, folded the wheelchair, and hoisted it into the back. It didn't quite fit, but with a piece of rope and a half-open trunk, it was a go. She got in.

"There! Isn't this lovely? We're getting to have a nice little ride just the two of us. What's the address?"

88

Wil swore under his breath. He hadn't worked it out that well after all. They would be reaching the trashcan he'd settled on in a few minutes. He had to make the call now. His co-worker Rinus sat next to him, humming along to "I'm Dreaming of a White Christmas" playing on the truck radio.

"Can you take care of the next can? I've got to make a call. My wife's sick."

Rinus looked up in surprise.

"You've got a cell phone now?"

"Yeah. I'm a bit worried about my wife."

That was strange, coming from Wil. He never talked about his wife, sick or not.

"Staff, what's up, bro? You're not yourself today."

"I'll explain later. Just go take care of the next can, all right?"

The two garbage men climbed out of the cab. Rinus ambled over to the can waiting to be emptied. Wil walked on a bit and took out his new prepaid cell phone and the slip of paper with the baby's parents' number on it, rehearsing his disguised voice one last time under his breath.

89

9:50 a.m.—Harry's Car

Harry glanced at the map he'd sketched of the garbage truck route his brother was driving that day. At the sanitation depot they'd looked a bit surprised when he'd walked in, harried and nervous, saying he needed to speak to his brother, Wil van Staveren, urgently.

"Family emergency," he'd told them.

When the building's manager had looked at him quizzically, he had said it again: "Something extremely serious. Family emergency."

After some hesitation, the man had shown him the notice-board in the canteen, and Harry had quickly jotted down the route Wil was driving that day. Without bothering to thank the manager, he had rushed out and jumped in his car.

A little later he realized he'd been a bit hasty, because he couldn't make heads or tails out of his own drawing. Now he was tearing around the neighborhood in a frenzy, in a haphazard attempt at catching up with a sanitation truck. At one point he thought he saw something that looked like one, but it turned out to be a Mini tricked out to look like a pickup truck.

Goddammit, Wil, where the hell are you?

In his mind's eye he could already picture himself in a prison cell. A two-person cell, cooped up with his brother.

There! This time he was sure. A truck with the city logo. He put his pedal to the metal, tore past the garbage truck, then squealed to a stop in front of it.

90

Graven plucked at his mustache as he spoke.

"So right this moment I've got a detective impersonating the father who's on his way to a trashcan in Breitner Street with a shopping bag full of cash. And ten of my guys in various disguises likewise on their way to that same location to catch the guy red-handed. So there's a good chance we'll very soon have the phony kidnapper in custody."

"At least that's *something*," the mayor couldn't stop herself from muttering. Even she was shocked at the way that sounded. "That's *great*," she added quickly.

It did not escape attorney Stork's notice.

"Still a bit disappointed, are you Simone, that the missing baby was recovered on its own? Without forceful measures on our part? Without a door-to-door search?"

Simone Schaarsberg Donk would not take the bait, but you could practically hear her teeth gnashing.

"Yeah, fortunately. Glad the whole operation fizzled out,"

the police chief said, innocently rubbing more salt in the wound.

"What time is the press conference?" she asked.

"We'll have to wait until the swindler's been caught."

"Of course, but I can't tell my press officer that."

Mathieu Stork suggested that the press officer should say she couldn't reveal what time the press conference would take place "in the interest of the ongoing investigation." He said it, head cocked sideways, somewhat roguishly.

Simone Schaarsberg Donk was fit to be tied.

91

9:51 a.m.—Garbage Truck

Wil launched a string of profanities at the idiot who'd squealed to a stop right in front of him, making him slam on his own brakes. He was halfway through a litany of fatal illnesses he wished upon the other driver, when he suddenly saw his brother Harry getting out of the car blocking his way.

"What the fuck, Harry. What are you doing here?"

Rinus, next to him, was looking a bit dazed. His forehead had slammed into the windshield, and he touched it gingerly to feel if it was bleeding. Then he turned and looked at Wil: "Do you know that moron?"

"That's my brother."

"Nice brother you've got!"

Harry, meanwhile, was gesturing wildly for Wil to come and speak to him. Wil jumped out of the cab; Rinus wanted to come too, but Wil pushed him back inside.

"*I'm* gonna have a word with him. Alone. Not you."

Rebuffed, Rinus sat back down in the passenger seat.

Harry dragged Wil over to where they wouldn't be overheard.

"What's the matter, man, you're fucking up the whole plan."

"The baby's back."

"Huh?"

"The kidnapped baby's been returned. Where is that ransom money?"

"I'm on my way to collect it. Here, at the end of the street, around the next corner."

"Well, you'd better leave it there. They're waiting for you."

It began slowly to dawn on Wil that while the largest sum of money he ever would have seen in his life was just one minute away from where he stood (he could almost feel the new fifty-euro bills crackling between his fingers: beer money, money for a new TV, a new car, and an Ajax season ticket), he would have to make a right turn instead of a left at the end of the street, and leave a hundred thousand euros sitting in a trashcan. Tears sprang to his eyes.

Harry too was sick at heart. He was seeing his spanking new RV go up in smoke.

"Hey, are we staying here all day, or what?" yelled Rinus from the truck.

Wil stomped back to his driver's seat, started the engine, and stepped on the gas. At the next corner he turned right. To his left, in the distance, he saw the trashcan containing his dreams. He even thought he could spy a corner of an Albert Heijn shopping bag sticking out of it.

"Hey, Staffie, you're going the wrong way."

"No, we're going back to the depot now, and you can just shut your big trap."

Rinus, startled, looked at him, and for once he was unable to come up with a sassy retort.

92

"Could you tell us why it took so long for you to announce the baby was back safe and sound?" the correspondent from *RTL Boulevard* asked.

The municipal press officer glanced at the mayor. Who nodded sourly.

"We suspected there might be others involved in the kidnapping, and we were trying to catch them as well," the information officer said.

"Were they demanding a ransom, and if so, did you catch the crook or crooks?" another reporter asked.

The press officer looked at the mayor again.

"In view of the ongoing investigation we have no comment at this time."

93

Same Time—Evert's House

Seated on the old three-person sofa in front of the television, Rita, Jenny, and I were contentedly watching the news, each with a glass of mock champagne in one hand and an eclair in the other. The local station was broadcasting the press conference live.

"Ransom? What the hell are they talking about?" Evert exclaimed, startled. He was reclining in his old leather armchair, his plaster cast resting on the coffee table in front of him. Mo was asleep next to his chair.

"Hey, Henkie, did you ask for a ransom without telling me?"

"No, I'm such a dope that it never even occurred to me," I replied.

Meanwhile the face of Chief Prosecutor Stork had popped up on the screen. A journalist asked if there were going to be any indictments.

"Hmm, I think that's unlikely," he answered, poker-faced.

A cheer went up in Evert's living room.

"Did you see that? Did you see that?" Rita cried. "He winked at the camera, I swear. What a darling."

Evert and I looked at Rita open-mouthed.

"Do you know that guy?" we asked, practically in unison.

Rita laughed a bit sheepishly. She hesitated.

"He's my husband."

My mind boggled, and Evert stared at Rita as if she'd just turned into a panda.

"I think I'm starting to get the picture, Rita," I said.

Evert shook his head. "Well, explain it, then, because I don't get it at all."

"That gentleman up there on the TV possessed some inside knowledge, which he used to send his wife out to help us. Am I right, Rita?"

"More or less. My Mathieu did a bit of nosing around, going over the tips that had been phoned in to the police."

"Wow." That was all Evert was able to come out with.

"Your lips are sealed, of course, gentlemen," Rita said sternly.

Evert and I nodded our heads so vehemently they almost fell off.

"Oh, look, look!" cried Jenny.

The TV anchor announced they were now switching over to the happy parents.

The camera zoomed in on a crib. All you could see was a tiny hand sticking out of the blanket, and some wisps of hair.

I had to swallow a couple of times. Evert emptied his glass in one gulp and was suddenly bothered by something in his eye.

★ ★ ★

Wil van Staveren wasn't following any of this. He cracked open his sixth beer and stared glassily out the window.

★ ★ ★

His brother Harry, cursing under his breath, was in the school gymnasium, taking down a pathetic little Christmas tree.

About the Author

Hendrik Groen started his pseudonymous diary on the literary website of *Torpedo* magazine. He says about his first novel: "There's not one sentence that's a lie, but not every word is true." *The Secret Diary of Hendrik Groen* has been translated into over thirty languages.

Reading Group Guide

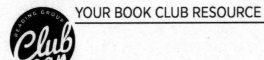 YOUR BOOK CLUB RESOURCE

Discussion Questions

1. Even though Hendrik is appalled by Evert's actions, he still helps his best friend conceal his misdeed and tries to return the baby. What would you have done in Hendrik's shoes? What are the limits of friendship?

2. *Two Old Men and a Baby* takes place prior to the events of *The Secret Diary of Hendrik Groen* and *On the Bright Side*. If you've read the other books in the Hendrik Groen series, how is Hendrik similar to and different from his older self? If you see differences in his personality, why do you think he might have changed as he got older?

3. What activity is Hendrik engaged in before Evert's arrival? How does this help characterize Hendrik?

4. What reason does Evert give for taking the baby stroller? Do you believe him? Can you think of any other possible explanations for his behavior?

5. Does this novel offer any commentary on society through the lens of Hendrik and Evert's misadventure?

6. After Evert shows up with the baby, Hendrik says to himself, "An hour ago my prime concern had been whether the Jenever was sufficiently chilled. Now my pal Evert was sitting in the living room with a baby on his lap that didn't seem to be in a mind to stop wailing any time soon" (page 54). What is Hendrik's attitude toward sudden life changes like this? Do you think his worldview is beneficial to him?

7. Discuss the conduct of the police throughout their investigation into the baby's disappearance. Do they ever cross lines of professionalism or legality? When police abuse their position of authority, how does this affect other people, and society as a whole?

8. The attempts of both Hendrik and Evert to return the baby and the authorities' efforts to find the baby are thwarted many times. What do you think are some of the reasons both parties fail in these objectives for most of the book?

9. Which characters display the greatest self-interest in the novel, and how does this impact events?

10. At one point, Evert says, "The environment's not my problem, I won't be alive to see it." and Hendrik responds, "But maybe Christina will" (page 76). Discuss each attitude and the motivations behind it. Where do you see these kinds of sentiments repeated in real life, and how do they impact our world?

YOUR
BOOK
CLUB
RESOURCE

VISIT
GCPClubCar.com

to sign up for the **GCP Club Car** newsletter, featuring exclusive promotions, info on other **Club Car** titles, and more.

 @grandcentralpub

 @grandcentralpub

 @grandcentralpub